THE LAST OF CHÉRI

Colette, the creator of Claudine, Chéri and Gigi, and one of France's outstanding writers, had a long, varied and active life. She was born in Burgundy in 1873, into a home overflowing with dogs, cats and children, and educated at the local village school. At the age of twenty she was brought to Paris by her first husband, the notorious Henry Gauthiers-Villars (Willy), writer and critic. By dint of locking her in her room, Willy forced Colette to write her first novels (the Claudine sequence), which he published under his name. They were an instant success. But their marriage (chronicled in *Mes Apprentissages)* was never happy and Colette left him in 1906. She spent the next six years on the stage - an experience, like that of her early childhood, which would provide many of the themes for her work. She remarried (*Julie de Carneilhan* 'is a close a reckoning with the elements of her second marriage as she ever allowed herself'), later divorcing her second husband, with whom she had a daughter. In 1935 she married Maurice Goudeket, with whom she lived until her death in 1954.

With the publication of *Chéri* (1920) Colette's place as one of France's prose masters became assured. Although she became increasingly crippled with arthritis, she never lost her intense preoccupation with everything around her. 'I cannot interest myself in anything that is not life,' she said; and, to a young writer, 'Look for a long time at what pleases you, and longer still at what pains you'. Her rich and supple prose, with its sensuous detail and sharp psychological insights, illustrates that personal philosophy.

Her writing runs to fifteen volumes, novels, portraits, essays, *chroniques* and a large body of autobiographical prose. She was the first woman President of the Académie Goncourt, and when she died was given a state funeral and buried in Père-Lachaise cemetery in Paris.

ALSO BY COLETTE

Fiction

Non-Fiction

Colette

THE LAST OF CHÉRI

TRANSLATED BY
Roger Senhouse

VINTAGE

Published by Vintage 2001

10 9

La Fin de Chéri first published in Paris 1926
First published in Great Britain by Gollancz, 1933
This translation published by
Martin Secker & Warburg, 1951

Vintage
Random House, 20 Vauxhall Bridge Road,
London SW1V 2SA

www.vintage-books.co.uk

Addresses for companies within The Random House Group Limited
can be found at:
www.randomhouse.co.uk/offices.htm

The Random House Group Limited Reg. No. 954009

A CIP catalogue record for this book
is available from the British Library

ISBN 9780099422778

The Random House Group Limited supports The Forest Stewardship
Council (FSC), the leading international forest certification organisation.
All our titles that are printed on Greenpeace approved FSC certified paper
carry the FSC logo. Our paper procurement policy can be found at:
www.rbooks.co.uk/environment

Printed and bound in England by
CPI Cox & Wyman, Reading, RG1 8EX

CHÉRI closed the iron gate of the little garden behind him and sniffed the night air: 'Ah! it's nice out here!' In the same breath, he changed his mind: 'No, it isn't.'

The thickly planted chestnut trees weighed heavily upon the heat pent up beneath. A dome of rusted leaves vibrated above the nearest gas-lamp. The Avenue Henri-Martin, close-set with greenery, was stifling; only with the dawn would a breath of fresh air come up from the Bois de Boulogne.

Bare-headed, Chéri turned back to look at the house, empty now but still lit up. He heard the clink of roughly handled glass, followed by the clear ring of Edmée's voice, sharp with reproof. He saw his wife come to the window of the gallery on the first floor and lean out. The frosted beads on her evening dress lost their snowy whiteness, caught for a moment a greenish glint from the lamp, then flamed into yellow as she touched the gold lamé curtains.

'Is that you on the pavement, Fred?'

'Who else could it be?'

'You didn't take Filipesco home, then?'

'No, I didn't; he'd hopped it already.'

'All the same, I'd rather have liked ... Oh well, it doesn't matter. Are you coming in now?'

'Not just yet. Far too hot. I'll just stretch my legs.'

'But ... Oh well, just as you like.'

She broke off a moment, and must have been laughing, for he could see the quiver of her frost-spangled dress.

'All I can see of you from here is a white shirt-front and a white face cut out on black. Exactly like a poster for a night-club. It looks devastating.'

'How you adore my mother's expressions!' he said reflectively. 'You can tell everyone to go to bed. I've got my key.'

She waved a hand in his direction. He watched the lights go out one by one in all the windows. One particular light – a dull blue gleam – told Chéri that Edmée was going through her boudoir into their bedroom, which looked out on the garden at the back of the house.

I

'The boudoir will soon come to be known as the study, and no mistake,' he thought.

The clock of Janson-de-Sailly began to strike and Chéri cocked his ear to catch the chiming notes in flight, like drops of rain. 'Midnight! She's in a hurry to get to bed. ... Yes, of course, she has to be at her Hospital by nine tomorrow morning.' He took a few nervous steps, shrugged his shoulders, and grew calmer.

'It's as if I'd married a ballet-dancer. Nine o'clock sharp, the class: it's sacrosanct. It has to come before everything else.'

He walked on as far as the entrance to the Bois. The day's dust, hanging in the pallid sky, dimmed the brightness of the stars. Step for step, a second tread echoed Chéri's: he stopped and waited for it to catch up with him. He disliked anyone walking behind him.

'Good evening, Monsieur Peloux,' said the night-watchman, touching his cap.

Chéri answered by raising a finger to his forehead with the condescension of an officer – a trick he had picked up during the war from his fellow quartermaster-sergeants – and walked on past the night-watchman, who was trying the locks on the iron gates to the little private gardens.

From a couple of lovers on a bench just inside the Bois came the rustle of crushed clothes and the whisper of smothered endearments. Chéri listened for an instant to the clasped bodies and invisible lips, a sound like the ripple of a ship's prow cleaving calm waters.

'The man's a soldier,' he noticed. 'I've just heard him unbuckle his belt.'

He was not thinking, which left his every sense on the alert. On many a calm night during the war Chéri had derived complex pleasure and subtle terror from his primitive keenness of hearing; his fingers, even when caked with mud and pocket fug, had been quick to distinguish the image on medal or coin, and to tell, by leaf or stalk, plants whose name he did not know. 'Hi, there, Peloux lad, just tell us what I've got a hold of here?' Chéri recalled the ginger-headed lad who, under cover of darkness, would push into his hand a dead mole, a small snake, a tree-frog, an over-ripe fruit, or some piece of filth, and then exclaim, 'Blimey, he gets it every time!' The memory made him smile, but with no pity for the ginger-headed lad, now dead. Yet he was haunted sometimes by the picture of his pal Pierquin, lying there on his back asleep for ever, with a look of distrust still on his face. He often spoke of him.

This very evening, at home, when dinner was over, Edmée had deftly steered the conversation round to the pathetic little tale, put together with such studied clumsiness. Chéri had it off by heart and it ended with the words: 'And then Pierquin said to me, "I had a dream about cats, old lad; and then I'd another dream about our river at home and it looked fair mucky. ... The meaning of that's pretty clear. ..." It was at this very moment he was picked off, by the smallest scrap of shrapnel. I wanted to carry him back. They found the two of us, him on the top of me, not a hundred yards from the spot. I tell you about him because he was a rare good sort ... and he had quite a lot to do with my being given this.'

And, as he ended on this modest note, Chéri had lowered his eyes to his green-and-red riband and knocked the ash off his cigarette, as though to keep himself in countenance. He considered it nobody's business that a chance explosion had thrown one of them across the other's shoulders, leaving Chéri alive and Pierquin dead. The truth – more ambiguous than falsehood – was that the terrific weight of a Pierquin, suddenly struck dead, had kept Chéri alive and half-suffocated, indignant and resentful. Chéri still bore a grudge against Pierquin. And, further, he had come to scorn the truth ever since the day when, years ago, it had suddenly fallen from his mouth like a belch, to spatter and wound one whom he had loved.

But at home this evening, the Americans – Majors Marsh-Meyer and Atkins, and Lieutenant Wood – had not appeared to listen to him. With the vacant faces of athletic first communicants, with fixed and expressionless eyes, they had simply been waiting to go to a night club, waiting with almost painful anxiety. As for Filipesco! 'Needs watching,' Chéri decided laconically.

The lake in the Bois was encircled with a fragrant mist that rose rather from the scythed slopes of its banks than from the stagnant water. Chéri was about to lean against a tree, when, from the shadows, a woman boldly brushed against him. 'Good evening, kid ...' The last word made him start; it was uttered in a low parched voice, the very voice of thirst, of dusty roads, of this dry hot night. ... He made no answer, and the dim figure came a step nearer on soft-soled shoes. But he caught a whiff of black woollens, soiled linen, dank hair, and turned back with long springy strides towards his own home.

The dull blue light was still on: Edmée had not yet left her boudoir study. In all probability she would still be seated at her desk, signing chits for drugs and dressings, reading through the day's notes and the short reports made by her secretary. Her pretty school-marm head, crimped hair with a reddish tint, would be bent over her papers.

Chéri pulled out the small flat key on the end of its thin gold chain. 'Here we go. In for another carefully measured dose of love. ...'

As was his habit, he entered his wife's boudoir without knocking. Edmée showed no sign of surprise, but went on with her telephone conversation. Chéri listened.

'No, not tomorrow. ... You won't want me there for that. The General knows you perfectly well. And at the Ministry of Commerce, there's ... What do you mean? "Have I got Lémery?" No, certainly not! He's charming, but ... Hullo? ... Hullo? ...' She laughed, showing her small teeth. 'Oh come! that's going too far. ... Lémery makes up to every woman, provided she's not blind or lame. ... What? Yes, he's come in, he's here at my elbow. No, no, I'll be very discreet. ... Goodbye. ... See you tomorrow. ...'

A plain white wrap, the white of her pearl necklace, was slipping off one shoulder. She had taken the pins from her chestnut hair, which, slightly frizzed by the dry atmosphere, followed every movement of her head.

'Who was that?' Chéri asked, as she put back the receiver and turned to ask him:

'Fred, you'll let me have the Rolls tomorrow morning, won't you? It will look better for bringing the General back here to lunch.'

'What General?'

'General Haar.'

'Is he a Boche?'

Edmée frowned. 'Really, Fred, you're too old for such jokes! General Haar is coming to inspect my Hospital tomorrow. Then

4

he can go back to America and tell them all that my Hospital can compare with any effort of the sort over there. Colonel Beybert will be showing him round, and they'll both come back here for luncheon afterwards.'

Chéri took off his dinner-jacket and sent it flying in the direction of a chair.

'I don't give a damn! I'm lunching out.'

'What d'you mean. What's all this?'

A spasm of rage crossed Edmée's face; but she smiled, picked up the dinner-jacket with care, and changed her tone of voice. 'Didn't you ask me a moment ago who that was on the telephone? Your mother.'

Chéri collapsed into an armchair and said nothing. His features were set in their most beautiful and impassive mould. Over his forehead hovered an air of serene disapproval. This was apparent, too, on his lowered eyelids, faintly shadowed now at the approach of his thirtieth year, and on his mouth, which he was careful never to compress too tightly, keeping his lips gently apart as in sleep.

'You know,' Edmée continued, 'she wants Lémery, of the Ministry of Commerce, to do something about her three cargo-loads of leather. There are three ships filled with leather, at present held up in harbour at Valparaiso. There is something in the idea, you know! The only thing is that Lémery won't grant the necessary import licence ... at least, that's what he says. Do you know how much money the Soumabis offered your mother as a minimum commission?'

With a wave of the hand, Chéri brushed aside ships, leather, and commission.

'Not interested,' he said simply.

Edmée dropped the subject, and affectionately approached her husband.

'You will have luncheon here tomorrow, won't you? There'll probably be Gibbs – the reporter from *Excelsior*, who's going to photograph the Hospital – and your mother.'

Chéri shook his head with no sign of impatience.

'No,' he said. 'General Hagenbeck –'

'Haar.'

'... and a Colonel, and my mother in her uniform. Her tunic – what d'you call it? her jacket? – with its little leather buttons; her elastic uplift-belt; epaulettes; high colonel's collar and her chin cascading over ... and her cane. No, really, I don't pretend to be braver than I am. I'd rather go out.'

He was laughing quietly to himself, and his laugh seemed mirthless. Edmée put a hand, already trembling with irritation, upon his arm; but her touch was light.

'You can't mean that seriously?'

'Certainly I can. I shall go for lunch to *Brekekekex*, or somewhere else.'

'With whom?'

'With whom I choose.'

He sat down and kicked off his pumps. Edmée leant against a black lacquer cabinet and racked her brain for words to make him behave sensibly. The white satin front of her dress rose and fell in rhythm to the quickened pace of her breathing, and she crossed her hands behind her back like a martyr. Chéri looked at her with an air of pretended indifference. 'She really does look a lady,' he thought. 'Hair all anyhow, in her chemise, on her way to the bath – she always looks a lady.'

She lowered her eyes, caught Chéri's, and smiled.

'You're teasing me,' she said plaintively.

'No,' Chéri replied. 'I shan't lunch here tomorrow, that's all.'

'But why?'

He rose, walked as far as the open door into their room – which was in darkness and filled with night scents from the garden – and then came back to her.

'Because I shan't. If you compel me to explain myself, I shall speak out and perhaps be rude. You'll burst into tears, and "in your distress", as the saying goes, you'll let your wrap slip to the floor and ... and unfortunately it won't have the slightest effect on me.'

Another spasm of rage passed over his wife's features, but her much-tried patience was not yet exhausted. She smiled and shrugged the one bare shoulder peeping from under her hair.

'It's quite easy to *say* that it won't have any effect on you.'

He was walking to and fro, clad in nothing but his short white silk pants. All the time he was testing the elasticity of his instep and calf muscles, and kept rubbing his hand over the twin brown scars under his right breast, as if to preserve their fading hue. Lean, with less flesh on his body than he had had at twenty, at the same time in better shape and training, he liked to parade up and down in front of his wife as a rival rather than a lover. He knew himself to be the more perfect specimen and, as a connoisseur, could condescend to admire in her the slim hips, the small breasts, and the graceful, almost imperceptible lines which Edmée knew so well how to clothe in tubular frocks and slinky tunics. 'Are you fading away, then?' he would sometimes ask her, just for the fun of annoying her. He would watch her whole body writhe in anger, and note its sudden and unsuspected vigour.

This reply of his wife's was distasteful to him. He wanted her to look well-bred, and to be silent, if not unresponsive, in his arms. He came to a halt, puckered his brow, and looked her up and down. 'Pretty manners, I must say. Do you learn them from your Physician-in-charge? The war, Madame!'

She shrugged her bare shoulder.

'What a child you are, my poor Fred! It's lucky we're by ourselves. To go on at me like that just because of a little joke … which was really a compliment. And for you to try and teach me manners, you … you! And after seven years of marriage!'

'Where do you get the seven years from?'

He sat down, naked as he was, as though for a prolonged discussion, his legs wide apart with all the ostentation of an athlete.

'Well … really … nineteen-thirteen … nineteen-nineteen …'

'Excuse me! it's clear that we don't reckon by the same calendar. Now, I count from …'

Edmée arched a knee, taking the weight of her body on the other leg, a confession of her weariness; but Chéri interrupted her with: 'Where's all this talk leading us? Come on, let's go to bed. You've got your ballet-class at nine tomorrow, haven't you?'

'Oh! Fred!'

Edmée crushed a rose from a black vase and threw away its petals. Chéri fanned the flames of anger still smouldering in her eyes, now moist with tears, by saying: 'That's the name I give that job-lot of wounded, when I'm not thinking.'

Without looking at him she murmured through trembling lips: 'You brute ... you brute ... you loathsome monster!'

He laughed, quite untouched.

'What d'you want me to say? As far as you're concerned, we all know you're carrying out a sacred mission. But what about me? You might just as well *have* to go to the Opera every day and practise in the Rotunda, for all the difference it would make. That would leave me just as much ... just as much out of it. And those men I called your "job-lot", well, they're wounded, aren't they? wounded who are a little luckier than others, perhaps. I've got absolutely nothing to do with them either. With them, too, I'm ... out of it.'

She turned round to face him so impulsively that it made her hair fly out from her temples: 'My darling, don't be so unhappy! You're not out of it at all, you're above all that!'

He got up, drawn towards a jug of iced water, on the sides of which the moisture was slowly condensing into bluish tears. Edmée hurried forward: 'With or without lemon, Fred?'

'Without, thanks.'

He drank, she took the empty glass from his hands, and he went towards the bathroom.

'By the way,' he said. 'About that leak in the cement of the bathing-pool. It ought –'

'I'm having it seen to. The man who makes those glass mosaics happens to be a cousin of Chuche, one of my wounded, and he won't need to be asked twice, believe me.'

'Good.' Then, as he was moving away, he turned round. 'Tell me, this business of the Ranch shares we were talking about yesterday morning, ought we to sell or not? Supposing I went to see old Deutsch about them tomorrow morning, and had a chin-wag with him?'

Edmée gave a shriek of schoolgirl laughter.

'Do you think I waited for you about that? Your mother had a stroke of genius this morning, while we were giving the Baroness a lift home.'

'You mean that old La Berche woman?'

8

'Yes, the Baroness. Your mother, as you so elegantly put it, had a chin-wag with her. The Baroness is one of the original shareholders, and never leaves the Chairman of the Board alone for a moment –'

'Except to cover her face in flour.'

'Must you interrupt me the whole time? ... and by two o'clock, my dear, the whole lot had been sold – every bit of it! The little flare-up on the Bourse this afternoon – it lasted only a very short time – raked us in something like two hundred and sixteen thousand francs, Fred! That'll pay for piles of medicine and bandages. I wanted to keep the news till tomorrow, and then give you one of these topping note-cases. Kiss?'

He stood, naked and white-skinned, holding back the folds of the door-curtain, and looking closely at the expression on his wife's face.

'That's all very well ...' he said at last, 'but where do I come in?'

Edmée gave a mischievous shake of the head: 'Your power of attorney still stands, my love. "The right to sell, purchase, draw up, or sign an agreement made out in my name ... etcetera" – which reminds me, I must send the Baroness something as a souvenir.'

'A briar pipe,' said Chéri, after pretending to have given the matter his attention.

'No, don't laugh. The good soul is so valuable to us.'

'And who are "us"?'

'Your mother and me. The Baroness knows how to talk to the men in a way they understand. She speaks their language. She tells them rather risky stories, but in such a way ... They dote on her.'

The strangest of laughs trembled on Chéri's lips. He let go his hold on the dark curtain, and it fell back into place behind him, thus obliterating him completely, as sleep obliterates the figment of a dream. He walked along a passage dimly lit by a blue globe, without making a sound, like a figure floating on air; for he had insisted upon having thick carpets laid on every floor, from top to bottom of the house. He loved silence, and furtiveness, and never knocked at the door of the boudoir, which his wife, since the war, called her study. She showed no annoyance, and sensing Chéri's presence, never jumped when he came into the room.

He took a shower-bath without lingering under the cool water, sprayed himself with scent absent-mindedly, and returned to the boudoir.

He could hear the sound of someone rumpling the sheets in the bedroom next door, and the tap of a paper-knife against a cup on the bedside table. He sat down and rested his chin on his hand. On the little table beside him, he caught sight of the morrow's menu, duly made out for the butler, according to daily routine. On it he read: '*Homard Thermidor, Côtelettes Fulbert-Dumonteil, Chaudfroid de canard, Salade Charlotte, Soufflé au curaçao, Allumettes au Chester.*' ... 'No alteration required,' he murmured to himself. '*Six places.*' – 'Ah, yes, that I must alter.' He corrected the number, and once more cupped his chin in his hand.

'Fred, do you know what time it is?'

He did not answer the soft voice, but went into their room and sat down facing the bed. With one shoulder bare and the other half hidden by a wisp of white nightgown, Edmée was smiling, despite her tired state, aware that she looked prettier in bed than out. But Chéri remained seated, and once again cupped his chin in his hand.

'Rodin's *Penseur*,' said Edmée, to encourage him to smile or to move.

'There's many a true word spoken in jest,' he answered sententiously.

He pulled the folds of his Chinese dressing-gown closer over his knees and savagely crossed his arms.

'What the hell am I doing here?'

She did not understand, or had no wish to do so.

'That's what I'd like to know, Fred. It's two o'clock, and I get up at eight. Tomorrow's going to be another of those pleasant little days. ... It's unkind of you to dawdle like this. Do come along; there's a nice breeze rising. We'll go to bed with it on our faces, and imagine we're sleeping out of doors.'

He weakened, and hesitated only an instant before hurling his silk wrap to a far corner of the room, while Edmée switched out the remaining light. She nestled up against him in the dark, but he neatly turned her over with her back to him and held her round the waist with strong arms, murmuring, 'Like that. That's like being on a bob-sleigh,' and fell asleep.

The following day, from the little window of the linen-room where he was hidden, he watched them leave. The duck's-egg-green motor and another long American automobile were purring very quietly in the avenue under the thick overhanging chestnut trees. The green shade and the recently watered pavement exuded a pretence of freshness, but Chéri knew very well that in the garden at the back of the house the heat of this June morning – the month that scorches Paris – was already shrivelling the lovely deep blue of a pool of forget-me-nots within their edging of pinks.

His heart began to beat with a sort of nervousness when he saw, approaching the iron gates to his house, two figures in khaki, with gold stars on their breast and crimson velvet bands round their caps.

'In uniform, of course, the crackpot!'

This was the nickname Chéri had bestowed on the Physician-in-Charge at Edmée's Hospital, and without really knowing it, he loathed the man and his red-gold hair and the caressing tones he put into technical terms when talking to Edmée. He muttered vague hearty curses, against the Medical Corps in particular, and against all who insisted on wearing uniform in peace-time. The American officer was growing fat, so Chéri sneered: 'I thought the Americans went in for sport. What's he doing with a belly like that?' but he said not a word when Edmée, in a white dress and white shoes, vivaciously held out her white-gloved hand to the Doctor. She greeted him in loud, quick, cheerful tones. Chéri had not missed a single word that fell from her red mouth, which parted in a smile over such tiny teeth. She had walked out as far as the motors, come back to tell a footman to fetch a notebook she had forgotten, and stood chatting while she waited for it. She had spoken in English to the American Colonel, and lowered her voice, in automatic deference, when replying to Doctor Arnaud.

Chéri was keeping a sharp look-out from behind the muslin curtains. His characteristic mistrust and slyness froze his features into immobility directly he concealed a strong emotion, and he kept a strict watch on himself, even when alone. His eyes travelled from Edmée to the Doctor, and then from the American Colonel back to Edmée, who had more than once looked up to the first floor, as though she knew of his hiding-place.

'What are they waiting for?' he grumbled under his breath. 'Ah, so this it is. ... God in heaven!'

Charlotte Peloux had arrived, in a sports-car driven by an impersonal and impeccable young chauffeur. Bursting out of her gabardine uniform, she held her head stiffly upright under its little tight-fitting hat with a military peak, and the ends of her bobbed red hair could be seen popping out at the back. She did not set foot to ground, but suffered them to come and pay their respects to her. She received Edmée's kiss and apparently asked after her son, for she too raised her head in the direction of the first floor, thus unveiling her magnificent eyes, over which drifted, as over the huge eyes of an octopus, some dark inhuman dream.

'She's wearing her little military cap,' Chéri murmured.

He gave a curious shudder, which made him angry with himself, and smiled when the three motors drove away. He waited patiently until his 'bachelor's runabout' drew up against the kerb punctually at eleven o'clock, and he kept it waiting for some considerable time. Twice he stretched out his hand to lift the receiver of the telephone, and twice he let it fall again to his side. His sudden impulse to invite Filipesco soon vanished and he thought he would like to collect young Maudru and his girl. 'Or, better still, Jean de Touzac. ... But at this hour he'll still be furiously snoring. Gosh! all that lot ... not one of them, I must be fair, a patch on Desmond. ... Poor old boy.'

He regarded Desmond as a war casualty; but with greater compassion than he ever vouchsafed the dead. Desmond, who was alive yet lost to him, had the power of inspiring him with an almost tender melancholy, as well as with the jealous respect due to a man with a 'job'. Desmond ran a night club, and sold antiques to Americans. A gutless wash-out during the whole of the war, when he had carried anything and everything but a rifle – official papers, billy-cans, any dirty hospital receptacle – Desmond had bitten deep into peace-time with a warlike fervour, and rich had been his immediate reward, very much to Chéri's astonishment. *Desmond's* had been started in quite a small way in a private house in the Avenue d'Alma, and now it sheltered frenzied and silent couples behind its heavy ashlar masonry, beneath ceilings decorated with swallows and hawthorn, and hemmed in by the bulrushes and flamingoes of its stained-glass windows. They danced at *Desmond's*, night and day, as people dance after war: the men, young and old, free from the burden of thinking and being frightened – empty-minded, innocent; the women, given over to a pleasure far greater than any more definite sensual delight, to the company of men: that is to say, to physical contact with them, their smell, their tonic sweat, the certain proof of which tingled in every inch of their bodies – the certainty of being the prey of a man wholly alive and vital, and of succumbing in his arms to rhythms as personal, as intimate, as those of sleep.

'Desmond will have got to bed at three, or three-thirty,' Chéri reckoned. 'He'll have had enough sleep.'

But once again he let drop the hand he had stretched out to the telephone. He went down the stairs in double-quick time, aided by the springy thick pile that covered every floorboard in his house. As he passed by the dining-room he looked without anger at the five white plates set in a diadem round a black crystal bowl, in which floated pink water-lilies, matching the pink of the tablecloth; and he did not pause till face to face with the looking-glass, fixed to the back of the heavy door of the reception-room on the ground floor. He feared, yet was attracted by, this looking-glass, which drew what little light it had from the french windows immediately facing it across the corridor, their opaque blue panes further obscured by the dark foliage of the garden. Every time he bumped into his own image, Chéri was brought up sharp by a slight shock when he recognized it as his own. He never could understand why this glass did not reflect the faithful image of a young man of twenty-four. He could not detect the precise points where time, with invisible finger, marks first the hour of perfection on a handsome face, and then the hour of that more blatant beauty, the herald of a majestic decline.

To Chéri's mind, there could be no question of a decline, and he could never have noticed it on his own features. He had just happened to bump into a thirty-year-old Chéri and failed to recognize him;

and he sometimes asked himself 'What's wrong with me?' as though he were feeling a little off-colour or had thrown his clothes on anyhow. Now he hurried past the reception-room door, and thought no more about it.

Desmond's, being a properly organized establishment, was up and doing by midday, despite the late hours it kept. The concierge was hosing the paved courtyard, a waiter was sweeping the steps clean, brushing away a heap of high-class rubbish – fine light dust, silver paper, corks with metal caps, stub-ends of gold-tipped cigarettes, and crumpled drinking-straws – rubbish which bore daily witness to the prosperity of *Desmond's*.

Chéri cleared at a bound the residue of last night's brisk business; but the smell inside the house barred further progress like a rope stretched across his path. Forty couples, packed like sardines, had left behind the smell – the memory of their sweat-soaked clothes – stale, and tainted with tobacco fumes. Chéri plucked up courage and leapt up the staircase, narrowed by heavy oak banisters supported on caryatids. Desmond had wasted no money on changing the stuffy sumptuosities of 1880. After removing two dividing walls, installing a refrigerator in the basement, engaging a jazz-band regardless of cost, no further outlay would be necessary for at least another year. 'I'll bring it up to date to attract customers', so Desmond said, 'when dancing isn't such a rage.'

He slept on the second floor, in a room where convolvulus ran riot on the walls and storks on the stained-glass windows; his bath was of enamelled zinc, bordered by a tiled frieze of river-plants, and the ancient heating apparatus wheezed like a bulldog past its prime. But the telephone shone as brightly as a weapon kept polished by daily use, and Chéri, after bounding up four steps at a time, discovered his friend, lips to the chalice, apparently imbibing the murky breath of its mouthpiece. His wandering glance came down to earth, and hardly settled on Chéri before it was off and up again to the convolvulus-wreathed cornice. His yellow-gold pyjamas cast a blight over a morning-after-the-night-before face, but Desmond was inflated by prosperity and no longer worried about being ugly.

'Good morning,' said Chéri. 'I came through all right. What a stench there is on your stairs. Worse than a dug-out.'

'... You'll never get *Desmond's* custom at twelve,' Desmond was saying to an invisible listener. 'I have no difficulty in buying Pommery at that price. And for my private cellar, Pommery ought to be eleven when minus labels ... hullo ... yes, the labels that came off in the general rumpus. That's what I want ... hullo?'

'You're coming out to lunch. I've got the runabout at the door,' Chéri said.

'No, and twice times no,' said Desmond.

'What?'

'No, and a thousand times no. Hullo? ... Sherry! What d'you take me for? This isn't a bar. Champagne, or nothing. Don't go on wasting your time and mine. Hullo. ... That's quite possible. Only I'm all the rage at the moment. Hullo. ... At two o'clock precisely. A very good day to you, Monsieur.'

He stretched himself before offering a limp hand. He still looked like Alfonso XIII, but thirty summers and the war had rooted this uncertain creature in the soil he needed. To have come through the war without firing a shot, to have eaten regularly, taken every advantage of it, and malingered in general, were so many personal victories from which he had emerged strengthened and self-confident. Assurance and a full pocket had made him less ugly, and you could be sure that, at sixty, he would give the illusion of having once passed for a handsome man with a large nose and long legs. He looked at Chéri condescendingly, but with a friendlier eye. Chéri turned away his head and said: 'What! Are you reduced to this? Come on, old boy. It's midday and you're not up yet.'

'In the first place, I *am* ready,' Desmond replied, unbuttoning his pyjamas to show a white silk shirt and a bronze-coloured bow tie. 'And in the second, I'm not going to lunch out.'

'So that's it,' said Chéri. 'Well, of all ... I'm speechless. ...'

'But if you like I can give you two fried eggs, and half my ham, my salad, my stout, and my strawberries. No extra charge for coffee.'

Chéri looked at him in impotent fury. 'Why?'

'Business,' said Desmond, with a deliberately nasal twang.

'Champagne! You heard what I was saying a moment ago. Oh! these wine-merchants! If one didn't put on the screw ... But I'm a match for them.'

He knotted his fingers and the knuckle-joints cracked with commercial pride.

'Yes or no?'

'Yes, you swine.'

Chéri chucked his soft felt hat at his head; but Desmond picked it up and brushed it with his forearm, to show that this was not the moment for childish jokes. They had eggs in aspic, ham and tongue, and good black stout with coffee-coloured foam on it. They spoke little, and Chéri, gazing out on to the paved courtyard, was politely bored.

'What am I doing here? Nothing, except that I'm not at home, sitting down to cutlets Fulbert-Dumonteil.' He visualized Edmée in white, the baby-faced American Colonel, and Arnaud, the Physician-in-Charge, in whose presence she acted the docile little girl. He thought of Charlotte Peloux's epaulettes, and a sort of fruitless affection for his host was coming over him, when the latter asked him an abrupt question:

'Do you know how much champagne was drunk here last night, between four o'clock yesterday and four o'clock this morning?'

'No,' said Chéri.

'And do you know how many bottles were returned empty from those delivered here between May the first and June the fifteenth?'

'No,' said Chéri.

'Say a number.'

'No idea,' Chéri grunted.

'But say something! Say a number! Have a guess, man! Name some figure!'

Chéri scratched the table-cloth as he might during an examination. He was suffering from the heat, and from his own inertia.

'Five hundred,' he got out at last.

Desmond threw himself back in his chair and, as it swerved through the air, his monocle shot a piercing flash of sunlight into Chéri's eye.

'Five hundred! You make me laugh!'

He was boasting. He did not know how to laugh: his nearest approach was a sort of sob of the shoulders. He drank some coffee, to excite Chéri's curiosity, and then put down his cup again.

'Three thousand, three hundred, and eighty-two, my boy. And do you know how much that puts in my pocket?'

'No,' Chéri interrupted, 'and I don't give a damn. That's enough. My mother does all that for me if I want it. Besides ...' He rose, and added in a hesitant voice: 'Besides, money doesn't interest me.'

'Strange,' said Desmond, hurt. 'Strange. Amusing.'

'If you like. No, can't you understand, money doesn't interest me ... doesn't interest me any more.'

These simple words fell from his lips slowly. Chéri spoke them without looking up, and kicked a biscuit crumb along the carpet; his embarrassment at making this confession, his secretive look, restored for a fleeting instant the full marvel of his youth.

For the first time Desmond stared at him with the critical attention of a doctor examining a patient, 'Am I dealing with a malingerer?' Like a doctor, he had recourse to confused and soothing words.

'We all go through that. Everyone's feeling a little out of sorts. No one knows exactly where he stands. Work is a wonderful way of putting you on your feet again, old boy. Take me, for instance. ...'

'I know,' Chéri interrupted. 'You're going to tell me I haven't enough to do.'

'Yes, it's your own fault.' Desmond's mockery was condescending in the extreme. 'For in these wonderful times ...' He was going on to confess his deep satisfaction with business, but he pulled himself up in time. 'It's also a question of upbringing. Obviously, you never learned the first thing about life under Léa's wing. You've no idea how to manage people and things.'

'So they say.' Chéri was put out. 'Léa herself wasn't fooled. You mayn't believe me, but though she didn't trust me, she always consulted me before buying or selling.'

He thrust out his chest, proud of the days gone by, when distrust was synonymous with respect.

'You've only got to apply yourself to it again – to money matters,' Desmond continued, in his advisory capacity. 'It's a game that never goes out of fashion.'

'Yes,' Chéri acquiesced rather vaguely. 'Yes, of course. I'm only waiting.'

'Waiting for what?'

'I'm waiting. ... What I mean is ... I'm waiting for an opportunity ... a better opportunity. ...'

'Better than what?'

'What a bore you are. An excuse – if you like – to take up again everything the war deprived me of years ago. My fortune, which is, in fact ...'

'Quite considerable?' Desmond suggested. Before the war, he would have said 'enormous', and in a different tone of voice. A moment's humiliation brought a blush to Chéri's cheek.

'Yes ... my fortune. Well, the little woman, my wife, now makes that her business.'

'Oh, no!' exclaimed Desmond, in shocked disapproval.

'Oh, yes, I promise you. Two hundred and sixteen thousand in a little flare-up on the Bourse the day before yesterday. So, don't you see, the question now arises, "How am I to interfere?" ... Where do I stand in all this? When I suggest taking a hand, they say ...'

'They? Who are "they"?'

'What? Oh, my mother and my wife. They start saying: "Take it easy. You're a warrior. Would you like a glass of orangeade? Run along to your shirt-maker, he's making you look a fool. And while you are going the rounds, you might call in and collect my necklace, if the clasp's been mended ..." and so on, and so forth.'

He was growing excited, hiding his resentment as best he could, though his nostrils were quivering, and his lips as well.

'So must I now tout motor-cars, or breed Angora rabbits, or direct some high-class establishment? Have I got to engage myself as a male nurse or accountant in that bargain basement, my wife's Hospital?' He walked as far as the window, and came back to Desmond precipitately. 'Under the orders of Doctor Arnaud, Physician-in-Charge, and pass the basins round for him? Must I take up this night-club business? Can't you *see* the competition!'

He laughed in order to make Desmond laugh; but Desmond, no doubt a little bored, kept a perfectly straight face.

'How long ago did you start thinking of all this? You certainly had no such ideas in the spring, or last winter, or before you were married.'

'I had no time for it,' Chéri answered quite simply. 'We went off on our travels, we began furnishing the house, we bought motors just in time to have them requisitioned. All that led up to the war. Before the war ... before the war I was ... a kid from a rich home. I was rich, damn it!'

'You still are.'

'I still am,' Chéri echoed.

He hesitated once more, searching for words. 'But now, it's not at all the same thing. People have got the jitters. And work, and activity, and duty, and women who serve their country – not half they don't – and are crazy about oof ... they're such thorough-going business-women that they make you disgusted with the word business. They're such hard workers it's enough to make you loathe the sight of work.' He looked uncertainly at Desmond. 'Is it really wrong to be rich, and take life easy?'

Desmond enjoyed playing his part and making up for past sub-servience. He put a protective hand on Chéri's shoulder.

'My son, be rich and live your own life! Tell yourself that you're the incarnation of an ancient aristocracy. Model yourself on the feudal barons. You're a warrior.'

'*Merde*,' said Chéri.

'Now you're talking like a warrior. Only, you must live and let live, and let those work who like it.'

'You, for instance.'

'Me, for instance.'

'Obviously, you're not the sort to let yourself be messed about by women.'

'No,' said Desmond curtly. He was hiding from the world a per-verse taste for his chief cashier – a gentle creature with brown hair scraped well back, rather masculine and hairy. She wore a religious medallion round her neck, and smilingly confessed, 'For two pins I'd commit murder: I'm like that.'

'No. Emphatically, no! Can't you mention anything without sooner or later dragging in "my wife, women", or else "in Léa's time"? Is there nothing else to talk about in 1919?'

Beyond the sound of Desmond's voice, Chéri seemed to be listening to some other, still unintelligible sound. 'Nothing else to talk about,' he repeated to himself. 'Why should there be?' He was daydreaming, lulled by the light and the warmth, which increased as the sun came round into the room. Desmond went on talking, impervious to the stifling heat, and as white as winter endive. Chéri caught the words 'little birds' and began to pay attention.

'Yes, I've a whole heap of amusing connexions, with whom, of course, I'll put you in touch. And when I say "birds", I'm speaking far too frivolously of what amounts to a unique collection, you understand, utterly unique. My regulars are tasty pieces, and all the tastier for the last four years. Just you wait and see, old boy! When my capital is big enough, what a restaurant I'll show the world! Ten tables, at most, which they'll fall over each other to book. I'll cover in the courtyard. ... You may be sure my lease provides for all additions I make! Cork-lino in the middle of the dance-floor, spotlights. ... That's the future! It's out there. ...'

The tango merchant was holding forth like a founder of cities, pointing towards the window with outstretched arm. Chéri was struck by the word 'future', and turned to face the spot indicated by Desmond, somewhere high up above the courtyard. He saw nothing, and felt limp. The reverberations of the two o'clock sun smote glumly down upon the little slate roof of the old stables, where the concierge of *Desmond's* had his lodging. 'What a ballroom, eh?' said Desmond with fervour, pointing to the small courtyard. 'And it won't be long now before I get it!'

Chéri stared intently at this man who, each day, expected and received his daily bread. 'And what about me?' he thought, inwardly frustrated.

'Look, here comes my swipes-merchant,' Desmond shouted. 'Make yourself scarce. I must warm him up like a bottle of Corton.'

He shook Chéri's hand with a hand that had changed its character: from being narrow and boneless, it had become broad, purposeful, disguised as the rather firm hand of an honest man. 'The war ...' thought Chéri, tongue in cheek.

'You're off? Where?' Desmond asked.

He kept Chéri standing on the top of the steps long enough to be able to show off such a decorative client to his wine merchant.

'Over there,' said Chéri, with a vague gesture.

'Mystery,' murmured Desmond. 'Be off to your seraglio!'

'Oh no,' said Chéri, 'you're quite wrong.'

He conjured up the vision of some female – moist flesh, nakedness, a mouth. He shuddered with impersonal disgust, and, repeating 'You're quite wrong' under his breath, got into his runabout.

He carried away with him an all too familiar uneasiness, the embarrassment and irritation of never being able to put into words all that he really wanted to say; of never meeting the person to whom he would have to confide a half-formed admission, a secret that could have changed everything, and which, for instance, this afternoon would have dispersed the ominous atmosphere from the bleached pavements and the asphalt, now beginning to melt under a vertical sun.

'Only two o'clock,' he sighed, 'and, this month, it stays light till well after nine.'

The breath of wind raised by the speed of his motor was like a hot dry towel being flapped in his face, and he yearned for the make-believe night behind his blue curtains, to the accompaniment of the simple drip-drop-drip of the Italian fountain's sing-song in the garden.

'If I slip quickly through the hall, I'll be able to get in again without being seen. *They'll* be having coffee by now.'

He could almost catch a whiff of the excellent luncheon, of the lingering smell of the melon, of the dessert wine which Edmée always had served with the fruit; and, ahead of time, he saw the verdigrised reflection of Chéri closing the door lined with plate glass.

'In we go!'

Two motors were dozing in the shade of the low-hanging branches just inside the gates, one his wife's and the other American, both in the charge of an American chauffeur who was himself taking a nap. Chéri drove on as far as the deserted Rue de Franqueville, and then walked back to his own front door. He let himself in without making a sound, took a good look at his shadowy form in the green-surfaced mirror, and softly went upstairs to the bedroom. It was just as he had longed for it to be – blue, fragrant, made for rest. In it he found every thing that his thirsty drive had made so desirable and more besides, for there was a young woman dressed in white, powdering her face and tidying her hair in front of a long looking-glass. Her back was turned to Chéri, and she did not hear him enter. Thus he had more than a moment to observe in the glass how flushed luncheon and the hot weather had made her, and to note her strange expression of untidiness and triumph and her general air of having won an emotionally outrageous victory. All at once Edmée caught sight of her husband and turned to face him without saying a word. She examined him critically from top to toe, waiting for him to speak first.

Through the half-open window facing the garden floated up the baritone notes of Doctor Arnaud's voice, singing, 'Oy Marie, Oy Marie'.

Edmée's whole body seemed to incline towards this voice, but she restrained herself from turning her head in the direction of the garden.

The slightly drunken courage visible in her eyes might well forebode a serious situation. Out of contempt or cowardice, Chéri, by putting a finger to his lips, enjoined silence upon her. He then pointed to the staircase with the same imperative finger. Edmée obeyed. She went resolutely past him, without being able to repress, at the moment when she came closest to him, a slight twist of the hips and quickening of the step, which kindled in Chéri a sudden impulse to strike her. He leant over the banisters, feeling reassured, like a cat that has reached safety at the top of a tree; and, still thinking of punishing, smashing, and taking flight, he waited there, ready to be wafted away on a flood of jealousy. All that came to him was a mediocre little feeling of shame, all too bearable, as he put his thoughts into words, 'Punish her, smash up the whole place! There's better to do than that. Yes, there's better to do.' But what, he did not know.

Each morning for him, whether he woke early or late, was the start of a long day's vigil. At first he paid but scant attention, believing it to be merely the persistence of an unhealthy habit picked up in the army.

In December 1918, after putting his knee-cap out of joint, he had eked out in his bed at home a short period of convalescence. He used to stretch himself in the early morning and smile. 'I'm comfortable. I'm waiting for the time when I feel much better. Christmas this year is really going to be worth while.'

Christmas came. When the truffles had been eaten, and the holly twig dipped in brandy set alight on a silver platter, in the presence of an ethereal Edmée, very much the wife, and to the acclamations of Charlotte, of Madame de La Berche, and members of the nursing staff of the Hospital, together with a sprinkling of Romanian officers and athletic adolescent American colonels, Chéri waited. 'Oh, if only those fellows would go away! I'm waiting to go to sleep, head in the cool air and feet warm, in my own good bed!' Two hours later, he was still waiting for sleep, laid out as flat as a corpse, listening to the mocking call of the little winter owls in the branches – a challenge to the blue light of his unshuttered room. At last he fell asleep; but a prey to his insatiable vigilance from the peep of dawn, he began to wait for his breakfast, and gave utterance to his hearty impatience: 'What the hell do they think they're doing with the grub downstairs?' He did not realize that whenever he swore or used 'soldiers' slang', it always went with an affected state of mind. His jolliness was a method of escape. Breakfast was brought to him by Edmée; but in his wife's bustling movements he never failed to discern haste and the call of duty, and he would ask for more toast, or for another hot roll which he no longer really wanted, simply from a malicious wish to delay Edmée's departure, to delay the moment when he would once more, inevitably, resume his period of waiting.

A certain Romanian lieutenant used to be sent off by Edmée to look for concentrated disinfectant and absorbent cotton wool, or again to press a demand upon Ministers – 'What the government refuses point-blank to a Frenchman, a foreigner gets every time,' she affirmed. He used to bore Chéri stiff by cracking up the duties of a soldier, fit or nearly fit, and the paradisal purity of the Coictier Hospital. Chéri went along there with Edmée, sniffed the smells of antiseptics which relentlessly suggest underlying putrefaction, recognized a comrade among the 'Trench Feet', and sat down on the edge of his bed, forcing himself to assume the cordiality prescribed by war novels and patriotic plays. He knew well enough, all the same, that a man in sound health, who had come through unscathed, could

23

find no peer or equal among the crippled. Wherever he looked, he saw the fluttering white wings of the nurses, the red-brick colour of the faces and hands upon the sheets. An odious sense of impotence weighed upon him. He caught himself guiltily stiffening one of his arms as if held in a sling, or dragging one of his legs. But the next moment he could not help taking a deep breath and picking his way between the recumbent mummies with the light step of a dancer. He was forced reluctantly to reverence Edmée, because of her authority as a non-commissioned angel, and her aura of whiteness. She came across the ward, and, in passing, put a hand on Chéri's shoulder; but he knew that the desire behind this gesture of tenderness and delicate possession was to bring a blush of envy and irritation to the cheek of a young dark-haired nurse who was gazing at Chéri with the candour of a cannibal.

He felt bored, and consumed by the feeling of weariness that makes a man jib at the serried ranks of masterpieces before him as he is being dragged round a museum. The plethora of whiteness, thrown off from the ceiling and reflected back from the tiled floor, blotted out all corners, and he felt sorry for the men lying there, to whom shade would have been a charity, though no one offered it. The noonday hour imposes rest and privacy upon the beasts of the field, and the silence of deep woodland undergrowth upon the birds of the air, but civilized men no longer obey the dictates of the sun. Chéri took a few steps towards his wife, with the intention of saying: 'Draw the curtains, install a punkah, take away that macaroni from the poor wretch who's blinking his eyes and breathing so heavily, and let him eat his food when the sun goes down. Give them shade, let them have any colour you like, but not always and everywhere this eternal white.' With the arrival of Doctor Arnaud, he lost his inclination to give advice and make himself useful.

The Doctor, with his white linen belly and his red-gold hair, had taken no more than three steps across the ward, before the hovering non-commissioned angel glided to earth again, to minister as a humble seraph, rosy with faith and zeal. Chéri thereupon turned to Filipesco, who was distributing American cigarettes, shouted 'Are you coming?' in contemptuous tones, and bore him away; but not before he had bidden farewell to his wife, to Doctor Arnaud, to nurses male and female, with the haughty affability of an official visitor. He crossed the rough gravel of the little courtyard, got into his car, and allowed himself no more than a dozen words' soliloquy: 'It's the regular thing. The correct move for the Physician-in-Charge.'

Never again did he cross the threshold of the Hospital, and thereafter Edmée invited him on State occasions only, out of official courtesy, much as one might, at a dinner-party, politely offer the snipe to a vegetarian guest.

He was now given over to reflection, and a prey to idleness. Before the war his idleness had been so light and varied, with the resonant ring of a flawless empty glass. During the war, too, he had endured periods of inertia under military discipline, inertia modified by cold, mud, risk, patrols, and even, on occasion, a little fighting. Conditioned to indolence by his upbringing and the life of a sensual young man, he had watched, himself untouched, the fresh young vulnerable companions all round him pine away in silence, solitude, and frustration. He had witnessed the ravages inflicted on intelligent people by the lack of newspapers as if they were being deprived of a daily drug. Whereas he had relapsed into contemplative silence – like a cat in a garden at night – content with a short letter, a postcard, or a cunningly packed parcel, other men, so-called superior men, had appeared to him to be showing every symptom of ruinous mental starvation. Thus he had learned to take pride in bolstering up his patience, and had brooded over two or three ideas, over two or three persistent memories, as highly coloured as a child's, and over his inability to imagine his own death.

Time and again, throughout the war, on coming out of a long dreamless sleep or a fitful bout of spasmodically interrupted rest, he would awake to find himself somewhere outside the present time and, his more recent past sloughed off, restored to the days of his boyhood – restored to Léa. Later, Edmée would suddenly rise up from the past, distinct and clear in every detail, and this evocation of her form, no less than its almost immediate disappearance, had always put Chéri in good spirits. 'That gives me two of them,' he reckoned.

Nothing came to him from Léa; he did not write to her. But he received postcards signed by the crabbed fingers of old mother Aldonza, and cigars chosen by the Baroness de la Berche. Sometimes he dreamed of a long soft-wool scarf, as blue as a pair of blue eyes and with a very faint suggestion of the scent associated with it throughout long hours of warmth and slumber. He had loved this scarf and hugged it to him in the dark, until it had lost its fragrance and the freshness of the blue eyes, and he had thought of it no more.

For four years he had not bothered his head about Léa. Her trusty old cronies, had occasion arisen, would have forwarded news of any events in her life. He never imagined anything happening to her. What had Léa in common with sickness, or Léa with change?

In 1918 he could not believe his ears when the Baroness de La Berche casually mentioned 'Léa's new flat'.

'Has she moved, then?'

'Where have you sprung from?' the Baroness answered. 'The whole world knows it. The sale of her house to the Americans was a brilliant deal, you bet! I've seen her new flat. It's small, but it's very cosy. Once you sit down in it, you never want to get up again.'

Chéri clung to the words 'small, but cosy'. Unable to imagine anything different, he supplied an over-all rose-pink background, threw in that huge galleon of gold and steel – the bed with its lace rigging – and hung Chaplin's pearly-breasted nymph from some floating cloud.

When Desmond began looking about for a sleeping partner for his night club, Chéri had spasms of alarm and anxiety. 'The blackguard's certain to try and tap Léa, or get her mixed up in some fishy business ... I'd better tip her off on the telephone.' He did nothing of the sort, however. Telephoning to a discarded mistress is riskier far than holding out your hand in the street to a nervous enemy who tries to catch your eye.

He went on biding his time, even after surprising Edmée in front of the looking-glass, after that flagrant exhibition of over-excitement, flushed cheeks, and untidiness. He let the hours slip by, and did not put into words – and so accentuate – his certainty that a still almost chaste understanding existed between his wife and the man who had been singing *'Oy Marie!'* For he felt much lighter in spirit, and for several days stopped uselessly consulting his wrist-watch as soon as daylight began to fade. He developed the habit of sitting out under the trees in a basket-chair, like a newly arrived guest in a hotel garden. There he marvelled to see how the oncoming night blotted out the blue of the monkshood, producing in its stead a hazier blue into which the shapes of the flowers were fused, while the green of their leaves persisted in distinct clumps. The edging of rose-coloured pinks turned to rank mauve, then the colour ebbed rapidly and the July stars shone yellow between the branches of the weeping ash.

He tasted at home the pleasures enjoyed by a casual passer-by who sits down to rest in a square, and he never noticed how long he remained there, lying back with his hands dangling. Sometimes he gave a fleeting thought to what he called 'the looking-glass scene' and the atmosphere in the blue room when it had been secretly troubled by a man's sudden appearance, theatrical behaviour, and flight. He whispered over and over, with foolish mechanical regularity, 'That's one point established. That's what's called a point-t-established,' running the two words together into one.

At the beginning of July he bought a new open motor, and called it his Riviera Runabout. He drove Filipesco and Desmond out along drought-whitened roads, but returned to Paris every evening, cleaving alternate waves of warm and cool air, which began to lose their good smells the nearer the motor drew to Paris.

One day he took out the Baroness de La Berche, a virile companion, who, when they came to the barriers of the Octroi, raised her forefinger to the little felt hat pulled well down on her head. He found her agreeable, sparing of words, interested in wayside inns overgrown with wistaria, and in village wine-shops with their cellar-smell and wine-soaked sand. Rigid and in silence, they covered two hundred miles or more, without ever opening their mouths except to smoke or feed. The following day Chéri again invited Camille de La Berche with a curt 'Well, how about it, Baroness?' and whisked her off without further ado.

The trusty motor sped far afield through the green countryside, and came back at nightfall to Paris like a toy at the end of a string.

27

That evening, Chéri, while never taking his eye off the road, could distinguish on his right side the outline of an elderly woman, with a man's profile as noble as that of an old family coachman. It astonished him to find her worthy of respect because she was plain and simple, and when he was alone in her company for the first time and far away from town-life, it began to dawn on him that a woman burdened with some monstrous sexual deformity needs must possess a certain bravura and something of the dignified courage of the condemned.

Since the war this woman had found no further use for her unkindness. The Hospital had put her back in her proper place, that is to say, among males, among men just young enough, just tamed enough by suffering, for her to live serenely in their midst, and forget her frustrated femininity.

On the sly, Chéri studied his companion's large nose, the greying hairy upper lip, and the little peasant eyes which glanced incuriously at ripe cornfields and scythed meadows.

For the first time he felt something very like friendship for old Camille, and was led to make a poignant comparison: 'She is alone. When she's no longer with her soldiers or with my mother, she's alone. She too. Despite her pipe and her glass of wine, she's alone.'

On their way back to Paris they stopped at a 'hostelry' where there was no ice, and where, trained against the plinths of columns and clinging to ancient baptismal fonts dotted about the lawn, the rambler-roses were dying, frizzled by the sun. A neighbouring copse screened this dried-up spot from any breeze, and a small cloud, scorched to a cherry hue, hung motionless, high in the heavens.

The Baroness knocked out her short briar pipe on the ear of a marble fawn.

'It's going to be grilling over Paris tonight.'

Chéri nodded in agreement, and looked up at the cloud. The light reflected from it mottled his white cheeks and dimpled chin, like touches of pink powder on an actor's face.

'Yes,' he said.

'Well, you know, if the idea tempts you, let's not go back till tomorrow morning. Just give me time to buy a piece of soap and a tooth-brush. ... And we'll telephone your wife. Then, tomorrow morning we can be up and on our way by four o'clock, while it's fresh.'

Chéri sprang to his feet in unthinking haste. 'No, no, I can't.'

'You can't? Come, come!'

Down near his feet he saw two small mannish eyes, and a pair of broad shoulders shaking with laughter.

'I didn't believe that you were still held on such a tight rein,' she said. 'But, of course, if you are ...'

'Are what?'

She had risen to her feet again, robust and hearty, and clapped him vigorously on the shoulder.

'Yes, yes. You run around all day long, but you go back to your kennel every night. Oh, you're kept well in hand.'

He looked at her coldly: already he liked her less. 'There's no hiding anything from you, Baroness. I'll fetch the car, and in under two hours we'll be back at your front door.'

Chéri never forgot their nocturnal journey home, the sadness of the lingering crimson in the west, the smell of the grasses, the feathery moths held prisoner in the beam of the headlamps. The Baroness kept watch beside him, a dark form made denser by the night. He drove cautiously; the air, cool at faster speeds, grew hot again when he slowed down to take a corner. He trusted to his keen sight and his alert senses, but he could not help his thoughts running on the queer massive old woman motionless at his right side, and she caused him a sort of terror, a twitching of the nerves, which suddenly landed him within a few inches of a wagon carrying no rear lamp. At that moment a large hand came lightly to rest on his forearm.

'Take care, child!'

He certainly had not expected either the gesture or the gentle tone of the voice. But nothing justified the subsequent emotion, the lump like a hard fruit stone in his throat. 'I'm a fool, I'm a fool,' he kept repeating. He continued at a slower speed, and amused himself by watching the refraction of the beams, the golden zigzags and peacock's feathers, that danced for a moment round the headlamps when seen through the tears that brimmed his eyes.

'She told me that it had a hold on me, that I was held well in hand. If she could see us, Edmée and me. ... How long is it since we took to sleeping like two brothers?' He tried to count: three weeks, perhaps more? 'And the joke about the whole business is that Edmée makes no demands, and wakes up smiling.' To himself, he always used the word 'joke' when he wished to avoid the word 'sad'. 'Like an old married couple, what! like an old married couple ... Madame and her Physician-in-Charge, Monsieur ... and ... his car. All the same, old Camille said that I was held. Held. Held. Catch me ever taking that old girl out again. ...'

He did take her out again, for July began to scorch Paris. But neither Edmée nor Chéri complained about the dog-days. Chéri used to come home, polite and absent-minded, the backs of his hands and the lower part of his face nut-brown. He walked about naked between the bathroom and Edmée's boudoir.

'You must have been roasted today, you poor townees!' Chéri jeered.

Looking rather pale and almost melting away, Edmée straightened her pretty odalisque back and denied that she was tired.

'Oh well, not quite as bad as that, you know. There was rather more air than yesterday. My office down there is cool, you know. And then, we've had no time to think about it. My young man in bed twenty-two, who was getting on so well ...'

'Oh yes!'

'Yes, Doctor Arnaud isn't too pleased about him.'

She didn't hesitate to make play with the name of the Physician-in-Charge, much as a player moves up a decisive piece on the chessboard. But Chéri did not bat an eyelid, and Edmée followed his movements, those of a naked male body dappled a delicate green from the reflected light of the blue curtains. He walked to and fro in front of her, ostentatiously pure, trailing his aura of scent, and living in another world. The very self-confidence of this naked body, superior and contemptuous, reduced Edmée to a mildly vindictive immobility. She could not now have claimed this naked body for her own except in a voice altogether lacking the stone and urgency of desire – that is, in the calm voice of a submissive mate. Now she was held back by an arm covered with fine gold hairs, by an ardent mouth behind a golden moustache, and she gazed at Chéri with the jealous and serene security of a lover who covets a virgin inaccessible to all.

They went on to talk about holidays and travelling arrangements, in light-hearted and conventional phrases.

'The war hasn't changed Deauville enough, and what a crowd ...' Chéri sighed.

'There's simply no place where one can eat a good meal, and it's a huge undertaking to reorganize the hotel business!' Edmée affirmed.

One day, not long before the Quatorze Juillet, Charlotte Peloux was lunching with them. She happened to speak of the success of some business deal in American blankets, and complained loudly that Léa had netted a half share of the profits. Chéri raised his head, in astonishment. 'So you still see her?'

Charlotte Peloux enveloped her son in the loving glances induced by old port, and appealed to her daughter-in-law as witness: 'He's got an odd way of putting things – as if he'd been gassed – hasn't he? ... It's disturbing at times. I've never stopped seeing Léa, darling. Why should I have stopped seeing her?'

'Why?' Edmée repeated.

He looked at the two women, finding a strange flavour in their kindly attention.

'Because you never talk to me about her ...' he began ingenuously.

'Me!' barked Charlotte. 'For goodness' sake ... Edmée, you hear what he says? Well at least it does credit to his feelings for you. He has so completely forgotten about everything that isn't you.'

Edmée smiled without answering, bent her head, and adjusted the lace that edged the low-cut neck of her dress by tweaking it between her fingers. The movement drew Chéri's attention to her bodice, and through the yellow lawn he noticed that the points of her breasts and their mauve aureoles looked like twin bruises. He shuddered, and his shudder made him realize that the conventional beauty and all the most secret details of her charming body, that the whole of this young woman, in fact, so close and so disloyal, no longer aroused in him anything but positive repugnance. Nonsense, nonsense; but he was whipping a dead horse. And he listened to Charlotte's ever flowing stream of nasal burblings.

'... and then again, the day before yesterday, I was saying in your presence, that motor for motor, well – I'd far rather have a taxi, a taxi, any day, than that prehistoric old Renault of Léa's – and if it wasn't the day before yesterday, it was yesterday, that I said – speaking of Léa – that if you're a woman living on your own and you've got to have a manservant, you might just as well have a good-looking one. And then Camille was saying, only the other day when you were there, how angry she was with herself for having sent a second barrel of Quarts-de-Chaumes round to Léa instead of keeping it for herself. I've complimented you often enough on your fidelity, my darling; I must now scold you for your ingratitude. Léa deserved better of you. Edmée will be the first to admit that!'

'The second,' Edmée corrected.

'Never heard a word of it,' Chéri said.

He was gorging himself with hard pink July cherries, and flipping them from beneath the lowered blind at the sparrows in the garden, where, after too heavy a watering, the flower-beds were steaming like a hot spring. Edmée, motionless, was cogitating on Chéri's comment, 'Never heard a word of it.' He certainly was not lying, and yet his off-hand assumed schoolboyishness, as he squeezed the cherry stones and took aim at a sparrow by closing his left eye, spoke clearly enough to Edmée. 'What can he have been thinking about, if he never heard a word?'

Before the war, she would have looked for the woman in the case. A month earlier, on the day following the looking-glass scene, she would have feared reprisals, some Red Indian act of cruelty, or a bite on the nose. But no ... nothing ... he lived and roamed about innocently, as quiet in his freedom as a prisoner in the depths of a gaol, and as chaste as an animal brought from the Antipodes, which does not bother to look for a kindred female in our hemisphere.

Was he ill? He slept well, ate according to his fancy – that is, delicately, sniffing all the meat suspiciously, and preferring fruit and new-laid eggs. No nervous twitch disfigured the lovely balance of his features, and he drank more water than champagne. 'No, he's not ill. And yet he's ... something. Something that I should guess, perhaps, if I were still in love with him. But ...' Once again she fingered the lace round the neck of her bodice, inhaled the warmth and fragrance that rose up from between her breasts, and as she bent down her head she saw the precious twin pink and mauve disks through the material of her dress. She blushed with carnal pleasure, and dedicated the scent and the mauve shadows to the skilful, condescending, red-haired man whom she would be meeting again in an hour's time.

'They've spoken of Léa in front of me every day, and I didn't hear. Have I forgotten her, then? Yes, I have forgotten her. But then what does it mean, "to forget"? If I think of Léa, I see her clearly, I remember the sound of her voice, the scent which she sprayed herself with and rubbed so lavishly into her long hands.' He took such a deep breath that his nostrils were indented, and his lips curled up to his nose in an expression of exquisite pleasure.

'Fred, you've just made the most horrible face; you were the spit and image of that fox Angot brought back from the trenches.'

It was the least trying hour of the day for the pair of them, awake and in bed with breakfast over. After a refreshing shower-bath, they were gratified to hear the drenching rain – three months ahead of the proper season – falling in sheets that stripped the false Parisian autumn of its leaves and flattened the petunias. They did not bother to find an excuse, that morning, for having wilfully remained behind in town. Had not Charlotte Peloux hit upon the proper excuse the previous evening? She had declared, 'We're all good Parigots, born and bred, aren't we! True blue one and all! We and the concierges can claim that we've had a real taste of the first post-war summer in Paris!'

'Fred, are you in love with that suit? You never stop wearing it. It doesn't look fresh, you know.'

Chéri raised a finger in the direction of Edmée's voice, a gesture which enjoined silence and begged that nothing should divert his attention while he was in the throes of exceptional mental labours.

'I should like to know if I have forgotten her. But what is the real meaning of "forgotten"! A whole year's gone by without my seeing her.' He felt a sudden little shock of awakening, a tremor, when he found that his memory had failed to account for the war years. Then he totted up the years and, for an instant, everything inside him stopped functioning.

33

'Fred, shall I never get you to leave your razor in the bathroom, instead of bringing it in here!'

Almost naked and still damp, he took his time in turning round, and his back was silver-flecked with dabs of talcum powder.

'What?'

The voice, which seemed to come from afar, broke into a laugh.

'Fred, you look like a cake that's been badly sugared. An unhealthy looking cake. Next year, we won't be as stupid as we have been this. We'll take a place in the country.'

'Do you want a place in the country?'

'Yes. Not this morning, of course.'

She was pinning up her hair. She pointed with her chin to the curtain of rain, streaming down in a grey torrent, without any sign of thunder or wind.

'But next year, perhaps ... Don't you think?'

'It's an idea. Yes, it's an idea.'

He was putting her politely at arm's length, in order to return to his surprising discovery. 'I really did think that it was only one year since I'd seen her. I never took the war into reckoning. I haven't seen her for one, two, three, four, five years. One, two, three, four. ... But, in that case, have I really forgotten her? No! Because these women have spoken of her in front of me, and I've never jumped up and shouted, "Hold on! If that's true – then what about Léa?" Five years ... How old was she in 1914?'

He counted once more, and ran up against an unbelievable total. 'That would make her just about sixty today, wouldn't it? ... How absurd!'

'And the important thing', Edmée went on, 'is to choose it carefully. Let's see, a nice part of the world would be –'

'Normandy,' Chéri finished for her absent-mindedly.

'Yes, Normandy. Do you know Normandy?'

'No ... Not at all well. ... It's green. There are lime trees, ponds ...'
He shut his eyes, as though dazed.

'Where do you mean? In what part of Normandy?'

'Ponds, cream, strawberries, and peacocks. ...'

'You seem to know a lot about Normandy! What grand country it must be! What else d'you find there?'

34

He appeared to be reading out a description as he leaned over the round mirror in which he made sure of the smoothness of chin and cheeks after shaving. He went on, unmoved, but hesitatingly. 'There are peacocks. ... Moonlight on parquet floors, and a great big red carpet spread on the gravel in front of ...'

He did not finish. He swayed gently, and slithered on to the carpet. His fall was checked half-way by the side of the bed. As his head lay against the rumpled sheets, the overlying tan of his pallid cheeks had the greenish tinge of an old ivory.

Hardly had he reached the floor when Edmée, without uttering a sound, threw herself down beside him. With one hand she supported his drooping head, and with the other held a bottle of smelling-salts to his nostrils, from which the colour was visibly ebbing. But two enfeebled arms pushed her away.

'Leave me alone. ... Can't you see I'm dying?'

He was not dying, however, and under Edmée's fingers his pulse retained its rhythm. He had spoken in a subdued whisper, with the glib, emphatic sincerity of very young would-be suicides who, at one and the same moment, both court death and fight shy of it.

His lips were parted over gleaming teeth and his breathing was regular; but he was in no haste to come right back to life. Safely ensconced behind his tightly shut eyes, he sought refuge in the heart of that green domain, so vivid in his imagination at the instant of his fainting fit – a flat domain, rich in strawberry-beds and bees, in pools of moonbeams fringed with warm stones. ... After he regained his strength, he still kept his eyes shut, thinking 'If I open my eyes, Edmée will then see the picture in my mind.'

She remained bowed over him on bended knee. She was looking after him efficiently, professionally. She reached out with her free hand, picked up a newspaper and used it to fan his forehead. She whispered insignificant but appropriate words, 'It's the storm. ... Relax. ... No, don't try to move. ... Wait till I slip this pillow under you. ...'

He sat up again, smiling, and pressed her hand in thanks. His parched mouth longed for lemons or vinegar. The ringing of the telephone snatched Edmée away from him.

'Yes, yes. ... What? Yes, of course I know it's ten. Yes. What?'

From the imperious brevity of her replies, Chéri knew that it was someone telephoning from the Hospital.

'Yes, of course I'm coming. What? In ...' With a rapid glance she estimated Chéri's term of recovery. 'In twenty-five minutes. Thanks. See you presently.'

She opened the two glass doors of the french windows to their fullest extent, and a few peaceful drops of rain dripped into the room, bringing with them an insipid river smell.

'Are you better, Fred? What exactly did you feel? Nothing wrong with your heart, is there? You must be short of phosphates. It's the result of this ridiculous summer we're having. But what can you expect?'

She glanced at the telephone furtively, as she might at an onlooker.

Chéri stood up on his feet again without apparent effort. 'Run along, child. You'll be late at your shop. I'm quite all right.'

'A mild grog? A little hot tea?'

'Don't bother about me. ... You've been very sweet. Yes, a little cup of tea – ask for it on your way out. And some lemon.'

Five minutes later she was gone, after giving him a look, which she believed expressed solicitude only. She had searched in vain for a true sign, for some explanation of so inexplicable a state of affairs. As though the sound of the door shutting had severed his bonds, Chéri stretched himself and found that he felt light, cold, and empty. He hurried to the window and saw his wife crossing the small strip of garden, her bead bowed under the rain. 'She's got a guilty back,' he pronounced, 'she's always had a guilty back. From the front, she looks a charming little lady. But her back gives the show away. She's lost a good half-hour by my having fainted. But "back to our muttons", as my mother would say. When I got married, Léa was fifty-one – at the very least – so Madame Peloux assures me. That would make her fifty-eight now, sixty perhaps. ... The same age as General Courbat? No! That's too rich a joke!'

He tried his hardest to associate the picture of Léa at sixty with the white bristling moustache and crannied cheeks of General Courbat and his ancient cab-horse stance. 'It's the best joke out!'

The arrival of Madame Peloux found Chéri still given over to his latest pastime, pale, staring out at the drenched garden, and chewing a cigarette that had gone out. He showed no surprise at his mother's entrance. 'You're certainly up with the lark, my dear mother.'

'And you've got out of bed the wrong side, it would seem,' was her rejoinder.

'Pure imagination. There are, at least, extenuating circumstances to account for your activity, I presume?'

She raised both eyes and shoulders in the direction of the ceiling. A cheeky little leather sports hat was pulled down like a vizor over her forehead.

'My poor child,' she sighed, 'if you only knew what I'm engaged on at this moment! If you knew what a gigantic task ...'

He took careful stock of the wrinkles on his mother's face, the inverted commas round her mouth. He contemplated the small flabby wavelet of a double chin, the ebb and flow of which now covered, now uncovered, the collar of her mackintosh. He started to weigh up the fluctuating pouches under her eyes, repeating to himself: 'Fifty-eight ... Sixty ...'

'Do you know the task I've set myself? Do you know?' She waited a moment, opening wider her large eyes outlined by black pencil. 'I'm going to revive the hot springs at Passy! *Les Thermes de Passy!* Yes, that means nothing to you, of course. The springs are there under the Rue Raynouard, only a few yards away. They're dormant; all they need is to be revived. Very active waters. If we go the right way about it, it will mean the ruination of Uriage, the collapse of Mont Dore, perhaps – but that would be too wonderful! Already I've made certain of the cooperation of twenty-seven Swiss doctors. Edmée and I have been getting to work on the Paris Municipal Council. ... And that's exactly why I've come – I missed your wife by five minutes. ... What's wrong with you? You're not listening to me. ...'

He persisted in trying to relight his damp cigarette. He gave it up, threw the stub out upon the balcony, where large drops of rain were rebounding like grasshoppers; then he gravely looked his mother up and down.

'I am listening to you,' he said. 'Even before you speak I know what you're going to say. I know all about this business of yours. It goes by the varying names of company promotion, wheezes,

37

commissions, founders' shares, American blankets, bully-beef, etcetera. ... You don't suppose I've been deaf or blind for the last year, do you? You are nasty, wicked women, that's all there is to it. I bear you no ill will.'

He stopped talking and sat down, by force of habit rubbing his fingers almost viciously over the little twin scars beneath his right breast. He looked out at the green, rain-battered garden, and on his relaxed features weariness battled with youth – weariness, hollowing his cheeks and darkening his eye-sockets, youth perfectly preserved in the ravishing curve and full ripeness of his lips, the downiness of his nostrils, and the raven-black abundance of his hair.

'Very well, then,' said Charlotte Peloux at length. 'That's a nice thing to hear, I must say. The devil turned preacher! I seem to have given birth to a Censor of Public Morals.'

He showed no intention of breaking the silence, or of making any movement whatever.

'And by what high standards do you presume to judge this poor corrupt world? By your own honesty, I don't doubt!'

Buckled into a leather jerkin, like a yeoman of old, she was at the top of her form and ready for the fray. But Chéri appeared to be through with all fighting, now and for ever.

'By my honesty? ... Perhaps. Had I been hunting for the right word, I should never have hit upon that. You yourself said it. Honesty will pass.'

She did not deign to reply, postponing her offensive until a later moment. She held her tongue that she might give her full attention to her son's peculiar new aspect. He was sitting with his legs very wide apart, elbows on knees, his hands firmly locked together. He continued to stare out at the garden laid flat by the lashing rain, and after a moment he sighed without turning his head: 'Do you really call this a life?'

As might be expected, she asked: 'What life?'

He raised one arm, only to let it fall again. 'Mine. Yours. Everything. All that's going on under our eyes.'

Madame Peloux hesitated a moment. Then she threw off her leather coat, lit a cigarette, and she too sat down.

'Are you bored?'

Coaxed by the unusual sweetness of a voice that sounded ethereally solicitous, he became natural and almost confidential.

'Bored? No, I'm not bored. What makes you think I'm bored? I'm a trifle ... what shall I say? ... a trifle worried, that's all.'

'About what?'

'About everything. Myself. ... Even about you.'

'I'm surprised at that.'

'So am I. These fellows ... this year ... this peace.' He stretched his fingers apart as though they were sticky or tangled in overlong hair.

'You say that as we used to say "This war" ...' She put a hand on his shoulders and tactfully lowered her voice. 'What is the matter with you?'

He could not bear the questioning weight of this hand; he stood up, and began moving about in a haphazard way. 'The matter is that everyone's rotten. No!' he begged, seeing an artificial look of indignation on the maternal countenance, 'No, don't start all over again. No, present company *not* excluded. No, I do *not* accept the fact that we are living in splendid times, with a dawn of this, a resurrection of that. No, I am *not* angry, don't love you any less than before, and there is nothing wrong with my liver. But I do seriously think that I'm nearly at the end of my tether.'

He cracked his fingers as he walked about the room, sniffing the sweet-smelling spray of the heavy rain as it splashed off the balcony. Charlotte Peloux threw down her hat and her red gloves, a gesture intended as a peace-offering.

'Do tell me exactly what you mean, child. We're alone.' She smoothed back her sparse hennaed hair, cut boyishly short. Her mushroom-coloured garb held in her body as an iron hoop clamps a cask. 'A woman. ... She has been a woman. ... Fifty-eight. ... Sixty ...' Chéri was thinking. She turned on him her lovely velvety eyes, brimming with maternal coquetry, the feminine power of which he had long forgotten. This sudden charm of his mother's warned him of the danger lying ahead, and the difficulty of the confession towards which she was leading him. But he felt empty and listless, tormented by what he lacked. The hope of shocking her drove him on still further.

'Yes,' he said, in answer to his own question. 'You have your blankets, your macaroni and spaghetti, your légions d'honneur. You joke about the meetings of the Chambre des Députés and the accident to young Lenoir. You are thrilled by Madame Caillaux, and by the hot springs at Passy. Edmée's got her shopful of wounded and her Physician-in-Charge. Desmond dabbles in dance-halls, wines and spirits, and white slavery. Filipesco bags cigars from Americans and hospitals, to hawk them round night clubs. Jean de Touzac ... is in the surplus store racket. What a set! What –'

'You're forgetting Landru,' Charlotte put in edgeways.

His eyes twinkled as he gave the slyest of winks, in silent tribute to the malicious humour that rejuvenated his old pugilist of a mother.

'Landru? That doesn't count, there's a pre-war flavour about that. There's nothing odd about Landru. But as for the rest – well ... well, to cut it short, there's not one who's not a rotter and ... and I don't like it. That's all.'

'That's certainly short, but not very clear,' Charlotte said, after a moment. 'You've a nice opinion of us. Mind you, I don't say you're wrong. Myself, I've got the qualities of my defects, and nothing frightens me. Only it doesn't give me an inkling of what you're really after.'

Chéri swayed awkwardly on his chair. He frowned so furiously that the skin on his forehead contracted in deep wrinkles between his eyes, as though trying to keep a hat on his head in a gusty wind.

'What I'm really after ... I simply don't know. I only wish people weren't such rotters. I mean to say, weren't *only* rotten. ... Or, quite simply, I should like to be able not to notice it.'

He showed such hesitancy, such a need of coming to terms with himself, that Charlotte made fun of it. 'Why notice it, then?'

'Ah, well. ... That's just the point, you see.'

He gave her a helpless smile, and she noticed how much her son's face aged as he smiled. 'Someone ought constantly to be telling him hard-luck stories,' she said to herself, 'or else making him really angry. Gaiety doesn't improve his looks ...' She blew out a cloud of smoke and in her turn allowed an ambiguous commonplace to escape her. 'You didn't notice anything of that before.'

He raised his head sharply. 'Before? Before what?'

'Before the war, of course.'

'Ah, yes ...' he murmured, disappointed. 'No, before the war, obviously. ... But before the war I didn't look at things in the same way.'

'Why?'

The simple word struck him dumb.

'I'll tell you what it is,' Charlotte chid him, 'you've turned honest.'

'You wouldn't think of admitting, by any chance, that I've simply remained so?'

'No, no, don't let's get that wrong.' She was arguing, a flush on her cheeks, with the fervour of a prophetess. 'Your way of life before the war, after all – I'm putting myself in the position of people who are not exactly broad-minded and who take a superficial view of things, understand! – such a way of life, after all, has a name!'

'If you like,' Chéri agreed. 'What of it?'

'Well then, that implies a ... a way of looking at things. Your point of view was a gigolo's.'

'Quite possibly,' said Chéri, unmoved. 'Do you see any harm in that?'

'Certainly not,' Charlotte protested, with the simplicity of a child. 'But, you know, there's a right time for everything.'

'Yes ...' He sighed deeply, looking out towards a sky masked by cloud and rain. 'There's a time to be young, and there's a time to be less young. There's a time to be happy ... d'you think it needed you to make me aware of that?'

She seemed suddenly to be upset, and walked up and down the room, her round behind tightly moulded by her dress, as plump and brisk as a little fat bitch. She came back and planted herself in front of her son.

'Well, darling, I'm afraid you're heading for some act of madness.'

'What?'

'Oh! there aren't so many. A monastery. Or a desert island. Or love.'

Chéri smiled in astonishment. 'Love? You want me ... in love with ...' He jerked his chin in the direction of Edmée's boudoir, and Charlotte's eyes sparkled.

'Who mentioned her?'

He laughed, and from an instinct of self-preservation became offensive again.

'*You* did, and in a moment you'll be offering me one of your American pieces.'

She gave a theatrical start. 'An American piece? Really? And why not a rubber substitute as provided for sailors into the bargain?'

He was pleased with her jingoistic and expert disdain. Since childhood he had had it dinned into him that a French woman demeans herself by living with a foreigner, unless, of course, she exploits him, or he ruins her. And he could reel off a list of outrageous epithets with which a native Parisian courtesan would brand a dissolute foreign woman. But he refused the offer, without irony. Charlotte threw out her short arms and protruded her lower lip, like a doctor confessing his helplessness.

'I don't suggest that you should work ...' she risked shamefacedly.

Chéri dismissed this importunate suggestion with a shrug of the shoulders.

'Work,' he repeated ... 'work, what you mean by that is hobnobbing with fellows. You can't work alone, short of painting picture postcards or taking in sewing. My poor mother, you fail to realize that, if fellows get my goat, women can hardly be said to inspire me either. The truth is, that I have no further use for women at all,' he finished courageously.

'Good heavens!' Charlotte caterwauled. She wrung her hands as though a horse had slipped and fallen at her feet; but harshly her son enjoined silence with a single gesture, and she was forced to admire the virile authority of this handsome young man, who had just owned up to his own particular brand of impotence.

'Chéri! ... my little boy! ...'

He turned to her with a gentle, empty, and vaguely pleading look in his eyes.

She gazed into the large eyes that shone with an exaggerated brilliance, due, perhaps, to their unblemished white, their long lashes, and the secret emotion behind them. She longed to enter through these magnificent portals and reach down to the shadowed heart which had first started to beat so close to her own. Chéri appeared to be putting up no defence and to enjoy being balked, as if under hypnosis. Charlotte had, in the past, known her son to be ill, irritable, sly; she had never known him unhappy. She felt, therefore, a strange kind of excitement, the ecstasy that casts a woman at a man's feet at the moment when she dreams of changing a despairing stranger into an inferior stranger – that is to say, of making him rid himself of his despair.

'Listen, Chéri,' she murmured very softly. 'Listen. ... You must ... No, no, wait! At least let me speak. ...'

He interrupted her with a furious shake of the head, and she saw it was useless to insist. It was she who broke their long exchange of looks, by putting on her coat again and her little leather hat, making towards the door. But as she passed the table, she stopped, and casually put her hand out towards the telephone.

'Do you mind, Chéri?'

He nodded his consent, and she began in a high-pitched nasal shrill like a clarinet. 'Hullo ... Hullo ... Hullo ... Passy, two nine, two nine. Hullo ... Is that you, Léa? But of course it's me. What weather, eh! ... Don't speak of it. Yes, very well. Everyone's very well. What are you doing today? Not budging an inch! Ah, that's so like you, you self-indulgent creature! Oh, you know, I'm no longer my own mistress. ... Oh no, not on that account. Something altogether different. A vast undertaking. ... Oh, no, not on the telephone. ... You'll be in all day then? Good. That's very convenient. Thank you. Goodbye, Léa darling!'

She put back the receiver, showing nothing but the curve of her back. As she moved away, she inhaled and exhaled puffs of blue smoke, and vanished in the midst of her cloud like a magician whose task is accomplished.

WITHOUT hurrying, he climbed the single flight of stairs up to Léa's flat. At six in the evening, after the rain, the Rue Raynouard re-echoed, like the garden of a boarding-school, with the chirrup of birds and the cries of small children. He glanced quickly, coldly, at everything, refusing to be surprised at the heavy looking-glasses in the entrance-hall, the polished steps, the blue carpet, or the lift-cage lavishly splashed with as much lacquer and gold as a sedan-chair. On the landing he experienced, for a moment, the deceptive sense of detachment and freedom from pain felt by a sufferer on the dentist's doorstep. He nearly turned away, but, guessing that he might feel compelled to return later, he pressed the bell with a determined finger. The maid, who had taken her time in coming to the door, was young and dark, with a butterfly cap of fine lawn on her bobbed hair: her unfamiliar face took from Chéri his last chance of feeling moved.

'Is Madame at home?'

The young servant, apparently lost in admiration of him, could not make up her mind.

'I do not know, Monsieur. Is Monsieur expected?'

'Of course,' he said, with a return of his old harshness.

She left him standing there, and disappeared. In the half-light, he was quick to take in his surroundings, with eyes blurred by the gloom, and alert sensitive nostrils. There was nowhere a vestige of that light golden scent, and some ordinary pine essence sputtered in an electric scent-burner. Chéri felt put out, like someone who discovers that he is on the wrong floor. But a great peal of girlish laughter rang out, its notes running down a deep descending scale. It was muffled by some curtain or other, but at once the intruder was cast into a whirlpool of memories.

'Will Monsieur please come to the drawing-room.'

He followed the white butterfly, saying over to himself as he went: 'Léa's not alone. She's laughing. She can't be alone. So long as it's not my mother.' Beyond an open door, he was being welcomed by rosy pink daylight and he waited, standing there, for the rebirth of the world heralded by this dawn.

A woman was writing at a small table, facing away from him. Chéri was able to distinguish a broad back and the padded cushion of a fat neck beneath a head of thick grey vigorous hair, cut short like his mother's. 'So I was right, she's not alone. But who on earth can this good woman be?'

'And, at the same time, write down your masseur's address for me, Léa, and his name. You know what I'm like about names. ...'

These words came from a woman dressed in black, also seated, and Chéri felt a preliminary tremor of expectation running through him: 'Then ... where is Léa?'

The grey-haired lady turned round, and Chéri received the full impact of her blue eyes.

'Oh, good heavens, child – it's you!'

He went forward as in a dream, and kissed an outstretched hand. 'Monsieur Frédéric Peloux – Princess Cheniaguine.'

Chéri bent over and kissed another hand, then took a seat.

'Is he your ...?' queried the lady in black, referring to him with as much freedom as if he had been a deaf-mute.

Once again the great peal of girlish laughter rang out, and Chéri sought for the source of this laugh here, there, and everywhere – anywhere but in the throat of the grey-haired woman.

'No, no, he isn't! Or rather, he isn't any longer, I should say. Valérie, come now, what are you thinking of?'

She was not monstrous, but huge, and loaded with exuberant buttresses of fat in every part of her body. Her arms, like rounded thighs, stood out from her hips on plump cushions of flesh just below her armpits. The plain skirt and the nondescript long jacket, opening on a linen blouse with a jabot, proclaimed that the wearer had abdicated, was no longer concerned to be a woman, and had acquired a kind of sexless dignity.

Léa was now standing between Chéri and the window, and he was not horrified at first by her firm, massive, almost cubic, bulk. When she moved to reach a chair, her features were revealed, and he began to implore her with silent entreaties, as though faced with an armed lunatic. Her cheeks were red and looked over-ripe, for she now disdained the use of powder, and when she laughed her mouth was packed with gold. A healthy old woman, in short, with sagging cheeks and a double chin, well able to carry her burden of flesh and freed from restraining stays.

'Tell me, child, where have you sprung from? I can't say I think you're looking particularly well.'

She held out a box of cigarettes to Chéri, smiling at him from blue eyes which had grown smaller, and he was frightened to find her so direct in her approach, and as jovial as an old gentleman. She called him 'child', and he turned away his eyes, as though she had let slip an indecent word. But he exhorted himself to be patient, in the vague hope that this first picture would give place to a shining transfiguration.

The two women looked him over calmly, sparing him neither goodwill nor curiosity.

'He's got rather a look of Hernandez ...' said Valérie Cheniaguine.

'Oh, I don't see that at all,' Léa protested. 'Ten years ago perhaps ... and, anyhow, Hernandez had a much more pronounced jaw!'

'Who's that?' Chéri asked, with something of an effort.

'A Peruvian who was killed in a motor accident about six months ago,' said Léa. 'He was living with Maximilienne. It made her very unhappy.'

'Didn't prevent her finding consolation,' said Valérie.

'Like anyone else,' Léa said. 'You wouldn't have wished her to die of it, surely?'

She laughed afresh, and her merry blue eyes disappeared, lost behind wide cheeks bulging with laughter. Chéri turned away his head and looked at the woman in black. She had brown hair and an ample figure, vulgar and feline like thousands and thousands of women from the south. She seemed in disguise, so very carefully was she dressed as a woman in good society. Valérie was wearing what had long been the uniform of foreign princesses and their ladies – a black tailor-made of undistinguished cut, tight in the sleeve, with a blouse of extremely fine white batiste, showing signs of strain at the breast. The pearl buttons, the famous necklace, the high stiff whalebone collar, everything about Valérie was as royal as the name she legitimately bore. Like royalty, too, she wore stockings of medium quality, flat-heeled walking shoes, and expensive gloves, embroidered in black and white.

From the cold and calculating way she looked him over, Chéri might have been a piece of furniture. She went on with her criticisms and comparisons at the top of her voice.

'Yes, yes, there is something of Hernandez, I promise you. But, to hear Maximilienne today, Hernandez might never have existed ... now that she has made quite certain of her famous Amerigo. And yet! And yet! I know what I'm talking about. I've seen him, her precious Amerigo. I'm just back from Deauville. I saw the pair of them!'

'No! Do tell us!'

Léa sat down, overflowing the whole armchair. She had acquired a new trick of tossing back her thick grey hair; and at each shake of the head, Chéri saw a quivering of the lower part of her face, which looked like Louis XVI's. Ostensibly, she was giving Valérie her full attention, but several times Chéri noticed a mischievous faltering in one of the little shrunk blue eyes, as they sought to catch those of the unexpected visitor.

'Well, then,' Valérie started on her story, 'she had hidden him in a villa miles outside Deauville, at the back of beyond. But that did not suit Amerigo at all – as you will readily understand, Monsieur! – and he grumbled at Maximilienne. She was cross, and said: "Ah! that's what the matter is – you want to be on view to the world and his wife, and so you shall be!" So she telephoned to reserve a table at the Normandy for the following evening. Everyone knew this an hour later, and so I booked a table as well, with Becq d'Ambez and Zahita. And we said to ourselves: "We're going to be allowed to see this marvel at last!" On the stroke of nine there was Maximilienne, all in white and pearls, and Amerigo. ... Oh, my dear, what a disappointment! Tall, yes, that goes without saying ... in point of fact, rather too tall. You know what I always say about men who are too tall. I'm still waiting to be shown one, just one, who is well put together. Eyes, yes, eyes, I've got nothing to say against his eyes. But – from here to there, don't you see' (she was pointing to her own face), 'from here to there, something about the cheeks which is too rounded, too soft, and the ears set too low. ... Oh, a very great disappointment. And holding himself as stiff as a poker.'

'You're exaggerating,' said Léa. 'The cheeks – well, what about cheeks? – they aren't so very important. And, from here to there, well really it's beautiful, it's noble; the eyelashes, the bridge of the nose, the eyes, the whole thing is really too beautiful! I'll grant you the chin: that will quickly run to flesh. And the feet are too small, which is ridiculous in a boy of that height.'

'No, there I don't agree with you. But I certainly noticed that the thigh was far too long in proportion to the leg, from here to there.'

They went on to thrash out the question, weighing up, with a wealth of detail and point by point, every portion of the fore and hind quarters of this expensive animal.

'Judges of pedigree fat cattle,' Chéri thought. 'The right place for them is the Commissariats.'

'Speaking of proportions,' Léa continued, 'you'll never come across anything to touch Chéri. ... You see, Chéri, you've come at just the right moment. You ought to blush. Valérie, if you can remember what Chéri was like only six, or say seven, years ago ...'

'But certainly, of course I remember clearly. And Monsieur has not changed so very much, after all. ... And you were so proud of him!'

'No,' said Léa.

'You weren't proud of him?'

'No,' said Léa with perfect calm, 'I was in love with him.'

She manoeuvred the whole of her considerable body in his direction, and let her gay glance rest upon Chéri, quite innocently. 'It's true I was in love with you, very much in love, too.'

He lowered his eyes, stupidly abashed before these two women, the stouter of whom had just proclaimed so serenely that she and he had been lovers. Yet at the same time the voluptuous and almost masculine tone of Léa's voice besieged his memory, torturing him unbearably.

'You see, Valérie, how foolish a man can look when reminded of a love which no longer exists? Silly boy, it doesn't upset me in the least to think about it. I love my past. I love my present. I'm not ashamed of what I've had, and I'm not sad because I have it no longer. Am I wrong, child?'

He uttered a cry, almost as if someone had trodden on his big toe. 'No, no, of course not! The very reverse!'

'It's charming to think you have remained such good friends,' said Valérie.

Chéri waited for Léa to explain that this was his first visit to her for five years, but she just gave a good-humoured laugh and winked with a knowing air. He felt more and more upset. He did not know how to protest, how to shout out loud that he laid no claim to the friendship of this colossal woman, with the cropped hair of an elderly cellist – that, had he but known, he would never have come upstairs, never crossed her threshold, set foot on her carpet, never collapsed in the cushioned armchair, in the depths of which he now lay defenceless and dumb.

'Well, I must be going,' Valérie said. 'I don't mean to wait for crush-hour in the Métro, I can tell you.'

She rose to face the strong light, and it was kind to her Roman features. They were so solidly constructed that the approach of her sixtieth year had left them unharmed: the cheeks were touched up in the old-fashioned way, with an even layer of white powder, and the lips with a red that was almost black and looked oily.

'Are you going home?' Léa asked.

'Of course I am. What d'you suppose my little skivvy would get up to if left to herself!'

'Are you still pleased with your new flat?'

'It's a dream! Especially since the iron bars were put across the windows. And I've had a steel grid fixed over the pantry fanlight, which I had forgotten about. With my electric bells and my burglar-alarms ... Ouf! It's been long enough before I could feel at all safe!'

'And your old house?'

'Bolted and barred. Up for sale. And the pictures in store. My little entresol flat is a gem for the eighteen hundred francs it cost me. And no more servants looking like hired assassins. You remember those two footmen? The thought of them still gives me the creeps!'

'You took much too black a view, my dear.'

'You can't realize, my poor friend, without having been through it all. Monsieur, delighted to have met you. ... No, don't you move, Léa.'

She enfolded them both in her velvety barbaric gaze, and was gone. Chéri followed her with his eyes until she reached the door, yet he lacked the courage to follow her example. He remained where he was, all but snuffed out by the conversation of these two women who had been speaking of him in the past tense, as though he were dead. But now Léa was coming back into the room, bursting with laughter. 'Princess Cheniaguine! Sixty millions! and a widow! – and she's not in the least bit happy. If that can be called enjoying life, it's not my idea of it, you know!'

She clapped her hand on her thigh as if it were a horse's crupper.

'What's the matter with her?'

'Funk. Blue funk, that's all. She's not the sort of woman who knows how to carry such wealth. Cheniaguine left her everything. But one might say that it would have done her less harm if he'd taken her money instead of leaving her his. You heard what she said?'

She subsided into the depths of a well upholstered armchair, and Chéri hated to hear the gentle sigh of its cushions as they took the weight of her vast bulk. She ran the tip of her finger along the grooved moulding of the chair, blew away the few specks of dust, and her face fell.

'Ah! things are not at all what they were, not even servants. Eh?'

He felt that he had lost colour, and that the skin round his mouth was growing tighter, as during a severe frost. He fought back an overwhelming impulse to burst out in rancour mingled with entreaties. He longed to cry out loud: 'Stop! Show me your real self! Throw off your disguise! You must be somewhere behind it, since it's your voice I hear. Appear in your true colours! Arise as a creature reborn, with your hair newly hennaed this morning, your face freshly powdered: put on your long stays again, the blue dress with its delicate jabot, the scent like a meadow that was so much a part of you. In these new surroundings I search for it in vain! Leave all this behind, and come away to Passy – never mind the showers – Passy with its dogs and its birds, and in the Avenue Bugeaud we'll be sure to find Ernest polishing the brass bars on your front door.' He shut his eyes, utterly worn out.

'And now, my child, I'm going to tell you something for your own good. What you need is to have your urine tested. Your colour's shocking, and you've got that pinched look round your lips – sure signs, both of them: you're not taking proper care of your kidneys.'

Chéri opened his eyes again, and they took their fill of this placid epitome of disaster seated in front of him. Heroically he said: 'D'you really think so? It's quite possible.'

'You mean, it's certain. And then, you've not got enough flesh on you. ... It's no use telling me that the best fighting cocks are scraggy. You could do with a good ten pounds more on you.'

'Give them to me,' he said with a smile. But he found his cheeks singularly recalcitrant and opposed to smiling, almost as though his skin had stiffened with age.

Léa burst into a peal of happy laughter, and Chéri tasted a pleasure which he could not have borne for long; he listened again to its full and rounded tones, the very laugh which in the old days used to greet some outrageous impertinence on the part of the 'naughty little boy'.

'That I could well afford! I've certainly been putting on weight, haven't I? Eh? Look ... here ... would you believe it? ... and again here!'

She lit a cigarette, exhaled a double jet of smoke through her nostrils, and shrugged her shoulders. 'It's age!'

The word flew out of her mouth so lightly that it gave Chéri a sort of extravagant hope. 'Yes: she's only joking. In a flash she'll reappear as her real self.' For an instant she seemed to take in the meaning of the look he gave her.

'I've changed a lot, haven't I, child? Fortunately, it doesn't much matter. As for you, I don't like the look of you at all. ... You've been fluttering your wings too much, as we used to say in the old days. Eh?'

He detested this new 'Eh?' with which she peppered her sentences so freely. But he stiffened at each interrogation, and each time mastered his rising excitement, preferring to remain in ignorance of both its reason and its aim.

'I don't ask whether you have any troubles at home. In the first place, it's none of my business; and besides, I know your wife as if I were her mother.'

He listened to the sound of her voice without paying much attention. He noticed, above all, that when she stopped smiling or laughing, she ceased to belong to any assignable sex. Despite her enormous breasts and crushing backside, she seemed by virtue of age altogether virile and happy in that state.

'And I know your wife to be thoroughly capable of making a man happy.'

He was powerless to hide his inward laughter, and Léa quickly went on to say:

'What I said was "a man", and not "any man". Here you are in my house, without a word of warning. You've not come, I take it, just to gaze into my beautiful eyes, eh?'

She turned on Chéri those once 'beautiful blue eyes', now so diminished, marbled with tiny red veins, quizzical, neither kind nor unkind, alert and bright certainly, but ... but where was now the limpid freshness that had laved their whites with palest blue? Where the contour of their orbs, with the roundness of fruit, breast, or hemisphere, and blue as a land watered by many a river?

Jestingly, he said, 'Pooh! aren't you sharp! A real detective!' And it amazed him to find that he had fallen into such a carefree posture, with his legs crossed, like a handsome young man with bad manners. For inwardly he was watching his other self, hopelessly distracted and on his knees, waving his arms, baring his breast, and shrieking incoherently.

'I'm not a particularly stupid woman. But you must admit that you don't present me today with a very difficult problem!'

She drew in her chin and its lower folds spread over her neck: the kneeling ghost of his other self bowed its head like a man who has received a death-blow.

'You show every known sign of suffering from the disease of your generation. No, no, let me go on. Like all your soldier friends, you're looking everywhere for your paradise, eh! the paradise they owe you as a war hero: your own special Victory Parade, *your* youth, *your* lovely women. ... They owe you all that and more, for they promised you everything, and, dear God, you deserved it. And what do you find? A decent ordinary life. So you go in for nostalgia, listlessness, disillusion, and neurasthenia. Am I wrong?'

'No,' said Chéri, for he was thinking that he would give his little finger to stop her talking.

Léa clapped him on the shoulder, letting her hand with its large rings rest there. As he bent his head down towards it, he could feel on his cheek the heat of this heavy hand.

'Oh!' Léa continued, raising her voice. 'You're not the only one! I've come across dozens of boys, since the war ended, exactly in your state of –'

'Where?' Chéri interrupted.

The suddenness of the interruption and its aggressive character put an end to Léa's parsonic eloquence. She withdrew her hand.

'They're to be met with everywhere, my child. Is it possible to be so vain? You seem to think you're unique because you find the post-war world insipid. Don't flatter yourself to that extent!'

She gave a low chuckle, and a toss to her sportive grey hair, and then a self-important smile like a judge who has a nice taste in wine. 'And you do flatter yourself, you know, always imagining that you're the only one of your kind.'

She took a step back and narrowed her gaze, adding, perhaps a little vindictively: 'You were unique only for ... for a time.'

Behind this veiled but carefully chosen insult, Chéri discovered something of her femininity at last. He sat bolt upright, delighted to find himself suffering less acutely. But by this time Léa had reverted to her milk and honey.

'But you didn't come here to have that said about you. Did you make up your mind on the spur of the moment?'

'Yes,' said Chéri.

He could have wished that this monosyllable might have been the last word between the two of them. Shyly, he let his gaze wander to all the things that surrounded Léa. From the nearest plate he took a dry cake shaped like a curved tile, and then put it back, convinced that it would turn to brick-red grit in his mouth were he to take a bite out of it. Léa noticed this action, and the painful way he swallowed his saliva.

'Tut, tut, so we're suffering from nerves, are we? Peeky chin, and dark lines under the eyes. That's a pretty state of affairs!'

He closed his eyes, and like a coward decided to listen and not look.

'Listen to me, child, I know a little restaurant in the Avenue des Gobelins. ...'

He looked up at her, in the full hope that she was going mad, that

53

in this way he would be able to forgive her for both looking and behaving like an old woman.

'Yes, I know a little restaurant ... Let me speak! Only, you must be quick, before the smart set and the newspapers take it into their heads to make it fashionable, and the good woman herself is replaced by a chef. She does all the cooking at present, and, my dear ...' She brought thumb and forefinger together on the tip of her lips, and blew an imitation kiss. Chéri turned away to look out of the window, where the shadow thrown by a branch flicked at the steady shaft of sunlight, impatiently but at regular intervals, much as a bent reed or river-plant appears to strike at the ripples of a regularly flowing current.

'What an odd sort of conversation ...' he ventured in strained tones.

'No more odd than your presence in my house,' Léa snapped back at him.

With a wave of the hand he made it clear that he wanted peace, only peace, with as few words spoken as possible, and preferably none at all. He felt defeated in face of this elderly woman's boundless reserves of energy and appetite. Léa's quick blood was now rising and turning her bulging neck and her ears to purple. 'She's got a crop like an old hen,' he thought, with something of his old enjoyment of cruelty.

'And that's the truth!' she hurled at him excitedly. 'You drag yourself round here, for all the world like an apparition, and when I do my best to find some way of putting things to rights, I who, when all's said and done, do happen to know you rather well ...'

He smiled at her despondently, 'And how in the world should she know me? When far shrewder people than she, and even than I myself ...'

'A certain kind of sickness of the soul, my child, of disillusion, is just a question of stomach. Yes, yes, you may laugh!' He was not laughing, but she might well think he was. 'Romanticism, nerves, distaste for life: stomach. The whole lot, simply stomach. Love itself! If one wished to be perfectly sincere, one would have to admit there are two kinds of love – well-fed and ill-fed. The rest is pure fiction. If only I knew how to write, or to make speeches, my child, what things I could say about that! Oh, of course, it wouldn't be anything new, but I should know what I was talking about, and that would be a change from our present-day writers.'

Something worse than this obsession with the kitchen was upsetting Chéri: the affectation, the false tone of voice, the almost studied joviality. He suspected Léa of putting on an act of hearty and sybaritic geniality, just as a fat actor, on the stage, plays 'jovial' characters because he has developed a paunch.

As though defiantly, she rubbed her shiny, almost blotchy red nose with the back of her first finger, and fanned the upper part of her body with the aid of the two revers of her long jacket. In so doing, she was altogether too cheerfully inviting Chéri to sit in judgement on her appearance, and she even ran her hand through her thick grey locks as she shook them free of her head.

'Do you like my hair short?'

He deigned to reply only by a silent shake of the head, just like someone brushing aside an idle argument.

'Weren't you saying something just now about a little restaurant in the Avenue des Gobelins ...?'

It was now her turn to brush aside an irrelevance. She was beginning to understand, and he could see from the quivering of her nostrils that at last she was piqued. His animal instincts, which had been shocked into dullness, were now on the alert and it was as though a weight had been lifted from his mind. He intended somehow to find a way past this shameless flesh, the greying curls, and 'merry friar' joviality, and reach the being concealed behind them, to whom he was coming back, as to the scene of a crime. He remained close to this buried treasure, burrowing towards it spontaneously. 'How in the world did old age come upon her? All of a sudden, on waking up one morning? or little by little? And this surplus fat, this extra avoirdupois, under the weight of which armchairs groan? Was it some sudden shock that brought about this change and unsexed her? Could it, perhaps, have been grief on my account?' But he asked these questions of no one but himself, and without voicing them. 'She is piqued. She's on the way to understanding me. She's just going to tell me. ...'

He watched her rise to her feet, walk over to the bureau, and start to tidy the papers lying on the open hinged flap. He noticed that she was holding herself more upright than when he had first entered the room, and that, under his following eye, she straightened her back still more. He accepted the fact that she was really colossal, her body seeming to run absolutely straight from armpit to hip. Before turning round again to face Chéri, she arranged a white silk scarf tightly round her neck, despite the heat of the room. He heard her take a deep breath, before she came towards him with the slow rolling gait of a ponderous animal.

She smiled at him. 'I am not doing my duty as a hostess, it would seem. It's not very polite to welcome someone by giving them advice, especially useless advice.'

From under a fold of her white scarf peeped insinuatingly a twisting, coiling, resplendent string of pearls, which Chéri at once recognized.

Held captive beneath the translucent skin, the seven colours of the rainbow flickered with some secret fire of their own all over the surface of each precious sphere. Chéri recognized the pearl with a dimple, the slightly egg-shaped pearl, and the biggest pearl of the string, distinguishable by its unique pink. 'These pearls, these at least, are unchanged! They and I remain unchanged.'

'So you've still got your pearls,' he said.

She was astonished by the foolish phrase, and looked as though she wanted to interpret it.

'Yes, in spite of the war. Are you thinking that I could, or should, have sold them? Why should I have sold them?'

'Or "for whom"?' he answered jokingly, in a tired voice.

She could not restrain a rapid glance towards the bureau and its scattered papers; and Chéri, in his turn, felt he knew the thought behind it, guessing that it was aimed at some yellowish postcard-photograph, probably the frightened features of a beardless boy in uniform. Disdainfully, he considered this imaginary face and said to himself, 'That's none of my concern,' adding a moment later, 'But what is there here that does concern me?'

The agitation which he had brought in his heart was now excited by everything around him; everything added to it – the setting sun, the cries of insect-chasing swallows, and the ember-glowing shafts of light stabbing through the curtains. He remembered that Léa carried with her wherever she went this incandescent rose-pink, as the sea, on its ebb-tide, carries with it far out from shore the earthy smells of pastures and new-mown hay.

No word passed between them for a while, and they were kept in countenance by pretending to listen to the clear fresh notes of a child singing. Léa had not sat down again. Standing massively in front of him, she carried her irretrievable chin higher than before, and betrayed some vague distress by the frequent fluttering of her eyelids.

'Am I making you late? Have you to go out this evening? Do you want to dress?' The questions were abrupt, and forced Léa to look at Chéri.

'Dress? Good Lord, and in what do you wish me to dress? I *am* dressed – irrevocably – once and for all.'

She laughed her incomparable laugh, starting on a high note and descending the scale by leaps of equal interval till she got to the deep musical reaches reserved for sobs and amorous moans. Chéri unconsciously raised a hand in supplication.

'Dressed for life, I tell you! And how convenient that is! Blouses, fine linen, and this uniform on top, and here I am in full fig. Equally ready for dinner either at Montagné's or somewhere modest, ready for the cinema, for bridge, or for a stroll in the Bois.'

'And what about love – which you're forgetting to mention?'

'Oh, child!'

She blushed: and, though her face was dark with the chronic red of sufferers from arthritis, the blush could not be concealed. Chéri, after the first caddish satisfaction of having said something outrageous, was seized with shame and remorse at the sight of this maidenly reaction.

'I was only joking,' he said, in some confusion. 'Have I gone too far?'

'Of course not. But you know very well I have never cared for certain kinds of impropriety or for jokes that are not really funny.'

She strove to control her voice, but her face revealed that she was hurt, and every coarsened feature gave signs of a distress that could perhaps be outraged modesty.

'Dear God, if she takes it into her head to cry!' and he imagined

57

the catastrophic effect of tears coursing down each cheek into the single deep ravine near the mouth, and of her eyelids reddened by the salt of tears.

He hastened to intercept: 'No, no, you mustn't think that! How could you! I never meant ... Please, Léa. ...'

From her quick reaction he realized suddenly that this was the first time he had spoken her name. Proud, as in the old days, of her self-control, she gently stopped him.

'Don't worry, child. I'm not offended. But I've only got you here for a few minutes, so don't spoil them by saying anything I shouldn't care to remember.'

Her gentle tone left him cold, and her actual words seemed offensively tactful to him. 'Either she's lying, or she really has become the sort of person she pretends. Peace, purity, and the Lord knows what! She might as well wear a ring in her nose! Peace of heart, guzzling, and the cinema. ... Lies, lies, all lies! She wants to make me think that women find growing old comfortable, positively enjoyable. How can she expect *me* to swallow that? Let her bore anyone else she likes with her fine talk about how cosy life is, and the little restaurants with the most delicious country dishes. I'm not having any! Before I could toddle, I knew all there is to know about reducing. I was *born* among ageing beauties! All my life I've watched them, my painted pixies, squabbling about their wrinkles, and, well into their fifties, scratching each other's eyes out over some wretched gigolo!'

'You sit there saying nothing, and I'm not used to it any more. I keep on thinking that there's something you want to say to me.'

On her feet, separated from Chéri by an occasional table with a decanter and port glasses, she made no effort to defend herself against the severe inspection to which she was being subjected; but from the almost invisible tremors that passed over her body, Chéri noted the muscular effort required to keep in her spreading stomach. 'How many times must she have put on her full-length corset again, left it off, then valiantly put it on again, before abandoning it for ever? ... How often of a morning must she have varied the shades of her face powder, rubbed a new rouge on her cheeks, massaged her neck with cold-cream and a small lump of ice tied up in a handkerchief, before becoming resigned to the varnished hide that now shines on her cheeks!' Impatience alone, perhaps, had made her tremble, yet this faint tremor led him to expect – so stubbornly blind was he to reality – some miraculous new blossoming, some complete meta-morphosis.

'Why don't you say something?' Léa persisted.

Little by little she was losing her poise, though she was careful not to move. She was playing with her rope of large pearls, knotting and unknotting, round her big well-manicured and wrinkled fingers, their luminous, indescribably bedewed and everlasting lustre.

'Perhaps it's simply because she's frightened of me,' Chéri mused. 'A man who says nothing must always seem a bit cranky. She's think-ing of Valérie Cheniaguine's terrors. If I put my hand out, would she scream for help? My poor Nounoune!' He lacked the courage to pronounce this name out loud, and, to protect himself from even a moment's sincerity, he spoke:

'What are you going to think of me?'

'It all depends,' Léa answered guardedly. 'At the moment you remind me of people who bring along a little box of cakes and leave it in the hall, saying to themselves: "There'll be plenty of time to produce these later," and then pick them up again when they go.'

Reassured by the sound of their voices, she had begun to reason like the Léa of old, quick on the uptake, and as wily as a sharp-witted peasant. Chéri rose to his feet, walked round the table which separ-ated him from Léa, and the daylight streaming through the pink curtains struck him full in his face. This made it easy for her to compute the passage of days and years from his features, which were all of them in danger, though still intact. There was something about so secret a falling away to tempt her pity and trouble her memory, and perhaps extract from her the word or gesture that would pre-cipitate Chéri into a frenzy of humiliation. As he stood there, a sacrifice to the light, with eyes lowered as if he were asleep, it seemed to him this was his last chance of extorting from her one last affront, one last prayer, one final act of homage.

Nothing happened, so he opened his eyes. Once more he had to accept the true picture – in the shape of his stalwart old friend, who, prudently keeping her distance, was bestowing on him a certain degree of benevolence from small and slightly suspicious blue eyes.

Disillusioned and bewildered, he looked all over the room for her, except in the very spot where she stood. 'Where is she? Where is she? This old woman is hiding her from me. She's bored by me, and she's waiting for me to go, thinking it all an infernal nuisance, these crowding memories and this returning ghost. ... But if by any chance I did ask for her help, if I beg her to give me back Léa ...' Deep inside him, his kneeling double was still palpitating, like a body from which the life-blood is being drained. With an effort of which he would never have deemed himself capable, Chéri tore himself away from this tortured image.

'I must be going,' he said out loud, and he added on a note of rather cheap wit, 'and I'm taking my box of cakes with me.'

Léa's exuberant bosom heaved with a sigh of relief. 'As you like, my child. But I'm always here, you know, if you're in any little trouble.'

Though she seemed so obliging, Chéri could sense an underlying resentment. Within that vast edifice of flesh crowned with silvery thatch, femininity had for a moment reasserted itself in tones resounding with an intelligent harmony. But Chéri could not respond: like a ghost he had come, and with the shyness of a ghost he must vanish, in his own despite.

'Of course,' Chéri replied, 'and I thank you.'

From that moment on, he knew, unerringly and spontaneously, exactly how to manage his exit. All the right words sprang to his lips, fluently, mechanically.

'You do understand, don't you, I came here today ... why not sooner, you may ask? I know I ought to have come a long while ago. ... But you will forgive me. ...'

'Of course,' Léa said.

'I'm even more hare-brained than before the war, you know, so that –'

'I understand, I understand.'

And because of this interruption, he thought that she must be impatient to see the last of him. A few words were exchanged during Chéri's retreat, in the intervals of bumping into some piece of furniture, crossing a strip of sunshine from the courtyard window – after the pink light in the drawing-room it seemed by comparison almost blue – kissing a puffy hand bulging with rings when it was raised to his lips. Another of Léa's laughs, which broke off abruptly half-way down its usual scale, just like a fountain when the jet is turned off and the crest of the plume, suddenly bereft of its stem, falls back to earth in a myriad separate pearls. ... The staircase seemed to glide away under Chéri's feet like a bridge connecting two dreams, and once more he was in the Rue Raynouard. Even the street was unfamiliar.

He noticed that the rosy tints of the sky were wonderfully reflected in the rain-filled gutters and on the blue backs of the low-skimming swallows. And now, because the evening was fresh, and because all the impressions he was bringing away with him were slipping back perfidiously into the recesses of his mind – there to assume their final shape and intensity – he came to believe that he had forgotten all about them, and he felt happy.

ONLY the sound of an old woman's bronchial cough, as she sat over her glass of crème-de-menthe, disturbed the peace of the bar room where the murmur of the Place de l'Opéra died away, as though muffled in an atmosphere too thick to carry any eddies of sound. Chéri ordered a long drink and mopped his brow: this precaution was a carry-over from the days when he had been a little boy and sat listening to the babble of female voices, as, with Biblical gravity, they bandied such golden rules as: 'If you want your milk of cucumber with real cucumber in it, you must make it yourself ...', or 'Never rub the perspiration into your face when you're overheated, or the perspiration will get under your skin and ruin it.'

The silence, and the emptiness of the bar, created an illusion of coolness, and at first Chéri was not conscious of the couple who, with heads bent close together across a narrow table, were lost in inaudible whisperings. After a few moments his attention was drawn to this unknown man and woman by an occasional hissing sibilant which rose above the main stream of their chatter, and by the exaggerated expressions on their faces. They looked like servants, underpaid, overworked, and patient.

He took a mouthful or two of the fizzy iced drink, leaned his head back against the yellow plush of the banquette, and was delighted to feel a slackening of the mental strain which, for the last fortnight, had been sapping his strength. The dead weight of the present had not accompanied him across the threshold of the bar, which was old-fashioned, with red walls, gilt festoons, plaster roses, and a large open hearth. The cloakroom attendant could be half seen in her tiled kingdom, counting every stitch as she mended the linen, her white hair bowed beneath a green lamp.

A passer-by dropped in. He did not trespass upon the yellow room, but took his drink standing at the bar as though to be discreet, and left without a word. The Odol odour of the crème-de-menthe was the only thing distasteful to Chéri, and he frowned in the direction of the dim old woman. Under a black and battered soft hat, he could distinguish an old face, accentuated here and there by rouge, wrinkles, kohl, and puffiness – all jumbled together – rather like a pocket into which have been popped, higgledly-piddledy, handkerchief, keys, and loose change. A vulgar old face, in short – and commonplace in its vulgarity, characterized, if at all, only by the indifference natural to a savage or a prisoner. She coughed, opened her bag, blew her nose vaguely, and replaced the seedy black reticule on the marble-topped table. It had an affinity with the hat, for it was made of the same black cracked taffeta, and equally out of fashion.

Chéri followed her every movement with an exaggerated repugnance; during the last two weeks he had been suffering, more than he could reasonably be expected to bear, from everything that was at once feminine and old. That reticule sprawling over the table almost drove him from the spot. He wanted to avert his eyes, but did nothing of the sort: they were riveted by a small sparkling arabesque, an unexpected brilliance fastened to the folds of the bag. His curiosity surprised him, but half a minute later he was still staring at the point of sparkling light, and his mind became an absolute blank. He was roused from his trance by a subconscious flash of triumphant certainty, and this gave him back the freedom to think and breathe. 'I know! It's the two capital Ls interlaced!'

He enjoyed a moment of calm satisfaction, not unlike the sense of security on reaching a journey's end. He actually forgot the cropped hair on the nape of that neck, the vigorous grey locks, the big nondescript coat buttoned over a bulging stomach; he forgot the contralto notes of the peal of youthful laughter – everything that had dogged him so persistently for the past fortnight, that had deprived him of any appetite for food, any ability to feel that he was alone.

'It's too good to last!' he thought. So, with a brave effort, he returned to reality. He looked more carefully at the offending object, and was able to reel off: 'The two initials, set in little brilliants, which Léa had designed first for her suède bag, then for her dressing-table set of light tortoise-shell, and later for her writing-paper!' Not for a moment would he admit that the monogram on the bag might represent some other name.

He smiled ironically. 'Coincidence be blowed! I wasn't born

yesterday! I came upon this bag by chance this evening, and to-morrow my wife will go and engage one of Léa's old footmen – again by chance. After that I shan't be able to go into a single res-taurant, cinema, or tobacconist's without running up against Léa at every turn. It's my own fault. I can't complain. I ought to have left her alone.'

He put some small change beside his glass, and got up before summoning the barman. He faced away from the old woman as he slipped between the two tables, holding himself in under his waist-coat, like a tomcat squeezing under a gate. This he managed so adroitly that the edge of his coat only just brushed against the glass of green crème-de-menthe. Murmuring an apology, he made a dash for the glass door, to escape into the fresh air beyond. Horrified, but not really in the least surprised, he heard a voice call out after him, 'Chéri!'

He had feared – known indeed – that this was coming. He turned to find that there was nothing about the raddled old ruin to help him recall her name; but he made no second attempt to escape, realizing that everything would be explained.

'Don't you recognize me? You don't? But how could you? More women were aged by the war than men were killed by it, and that's a fact. All the same, it's not for me to complain; I didn't risk losing anyone in the war. ... Eh! Chéri! ...'

She laughed; and recognition was complete, for he saw that what he had taken for decrepitude was only poverty and natural indiffer-ence. Now that she was holding herself upright and laughing, she did not look more than her age – sixty or thereabouts – and the hand with which she sought Chéri's was certainly not that of a doddering old grandmother.

'The Pal!' Chéri murmured, almost in tones of admiration.

'Are you really pleased to see me?'

'Oh, yes. ...'

He was not telling a lie. He was gaining assurance step by step and thinking, 'It's only her ... Poor Old Pal ... I'd begun to fear ...'

'Will you have a glass of something, Pal?'

'Just a whisky and soda, my pretty. My! haven't you kept your looks!'

He swallowed the bitter compliment which she tossed to him from the peaceful fringes of old age.

'And decorated, too,' she added out of pure politeness. 'Oh! I knew all about it, you may be sure! We all knew about it.'

The ambiguous plural failed to wrest a smile from Chéri, and the Pal thought she had shocked him.

'When I say "we", I'm speaking of those of us who were your real friends – Camille de La Berche, Léa, Rita, and me. You may be sure Charlotte would never have told me a word about it. As far as she's concerned, I don't exist. But – and I may as well say so – she doesn't exist for me, either.' She stretched out across the table a pale hand that had long forgotten the light of day. 'You must understand that Charlotte will never again be anything to me but the woman who contrived to get poor little Rita arrested and detained for twenty-four hours. ... Poor Rita, who had never known a word of German. Was it Rita's fault, I ask you, if she happened to be Swiss?'

'I know, I know. I know the whole story,' Chéri broke in precipitately.

The Pal raised her huge dark watery eyes towards him, full of inveterate complicity and a compassion that was always misplaced. 'Poor kid,' she sighed. 'I understand you. Forgive me. Ah! you've certainly had your cross to bear!'

He questioned her with a look, no longer accustomed to the overstatements that added a rich funeral tone to the Pal's vocabulary, and he feared she might be going to talk to him about the war. But she was not thinking of the war. Perhaps she never had, for it is the concern of two generations only.

She went on to explain. 'Yes, I was saying that to have such a mother must have been a heavy cross to bear for a son like you – for a boy, that's to say, with a blameless life, both before marriage and after! A nice, quiet boy and all that; not one to sow his wild oats all over the place, or to squander his inheritance.'

She wagged her head, and bit by bit he began to piece together the past. He rediscovered her, though she had the mask of a ravaged tragedy queen. Her old age was without nobility, yet bore no signs of illness, no tell-tale trace that betrayed her addiction to opium. The drug is merciful to those unworthy of it.

65

'Have you quite given up the pipe?' asked Chéri sharply.

She raised a white untended hand. 'What do you suppose? That kind of foolishness is all very well when you're not all on your own. In the days when I used to shock you young men, yes. ... You remember when you used to come back at nights? Ah! you were very fond of that. ... "Dear old Pal," you used to say to me, "just let me have another little pipeful, and pack it well!"'

Without turning a hair, he accepted this humble flattery, as he might from an old retainer, who fibs in order to fawn. He smiled knowingly, and scrutinized the folds of black tulle round her neck, looking in the shadows under the faded hat for a necklace of large fake pearls.

Almost mechanically and sip by sip, he drank the whisky which had been put in front of him by mistake. He did not care for spirits as a rule, but this evening he enjoyed the whisky, for it helped him to smile easily and softened to his touch unpolished surfaces and rough materials; it enabled him to listen kindly to an old woman for whom the present did not exist. They met again on the further side of the superfluous war-years and the young, importunate dead: the Pal spanned the gap by throwing across to Chéri a bridge of names – names of old men who bore charmed lives, of old women revitalized for the struggle or turned to stone in their ultimate shape, never to alter again. She recounted in detail a hard-luck story of 1913, some unhappiness that had taken place before August 1914, and something trembled in her voice when she spoke of La Loupiote – a woman now dead – 'The very week of your wedding, dear boy! you see what a coincidence it was? the hand of Fate was upon us, indeed' – dead after four years of a pure and peaceful friendship.

'We slanged each other day in, day out, dear boy, but only in front of other people. Because, don't you see, it gave them the impression that we were "a couple". Who would have believed it, had we not gone for each other hammer and tongs? So we called each other the most diabolical names, and the onlookers chuckled: "Have you ever seen such a devoted pair?" Dear boy, I'll tell you something else that will knock you flat – surely you must have heard about the will Massau was supposed to have made. ...'

'What Massau?' Chéri asked languidly.

'Oh, come. You knew him as well as you know yourself! The story of the will – so called – that he handed to Louise MacMillar. It was in 1909, and at the time I am speaking of, I was one of the Gérault pack, his pack of "faithful hounds" – and there were five of us he fed every evening at La Belle Meunière down at Nice; but on the Promenade des Anglais, you must remember, we only had eyes for you – dolled up in white like an English baby, and Léa all in white as well. ... Ah! what a pair you made! You were the sensation – a miracle, straight from the hands of the Creator! Gérault used to tease Léa: "You're far too *young*, girlie, and what's worse you're too proud. I shan't take you on for fifteen or twenty years at least. ..." And to think that such a man had to be taken from us! Not a tear at his funeral that wasn't genuine, the whole nation was in mourning. And now let me get on with the story of the will. ...'

Chéri was deluged with a perfect flood of incidents, a tide of bygone regrets and harmless resurrections, all declaimed with the ease and rapidity of a professional mourner. The two of them formed a symmetrical pattern as they leaned towards each other. The Pal lowered her voice when she came to the dramatic passages, giving out a sudden laugh or exclamation; and he saw in one of the looking-glasses how closely they seemed to resemble the whispering couple whose place they had taken. He got up, finding it imperative to put an end to this resemblance. The barman imitated his movement, but from afar, like a discreet dog when its master comes to the end of a visit. 'Ah! well ... yes ...' said the Pal, 'well, I'll finish the rest another time.'

'After the next war,' said Chéri jokingly. 'Tell me, those two capital letters. ... Yes, the monogram in little brilliants. ... It's not yours, Pal?'

He pointed at the black bag with the tip of his forefinger, extending it slowly while withdrawing his body, as though the bag were alive.

'Nothing escapes you,' the Pal said in admiration. 'You're quite right. She gave it to me, of course. She said to me: "Such bits of finery are far too frivolous for me nowadays!" She said: "What the devil do you suppose I'd be doing with those mirrors and powder and things, when I've a great face like a country policeman's?" She made me laugh. ...'

To stem the flood, Chéri pushed the change from his hundred-franc note towards the Pal. 'For your taxi, Pal.'

They went out on to the pavement by the tradesman's entrance, and Chéri saw from the fainter lamplight that night was coming on.

'Have you not got your motor?'

'My motor? No. I walked; it does me good.'

'Is your wife in the country?'

'No. Her Hospital keeps her in Paris.'

The Pal nodded her invertebrate hat. 'I know. She's a big-hearted woman. Her name's been put forward for a decoration, I understand from the Baroness.'

'What?'

'Here, stop that taxi for me, dear boy, the closed one. ... And Charlotte's going big guns in her support; she knows people round Clemenceau. It will make up a little for the story about Rita ... a little, not very much. She's as black as Sin itself, is Charlotte, my boy.'

He pushed her into the oven of the taxi, where she sank back and became enveloped in the shadow. She ceased to exist. It was as though he had never met her, now that he heard her voice no longer. He took stock of the night, filling his lungs with the dust-laden air that foretold another scorching day. He pictured, as in a dream, that he would wake up at home, among gardens watered every evening, among the scent of Spanish honeysuckle and the call of birds, resting alongside his wife's straight hips. ... But the Pal's voice rose up from the depths of the taxi: 'Two hundred and fourteen, Avenue de Villiers! Remember my address, Chéri! And you know that I often dine at the *Giraffe*, Avenue de Wagram, don't you, if ever you should want me. ... You know, if ever you should be looking for me.'

'That's really the limit,' thought Chéri, lengthening his step. ' "If I should ever be looking for her." I ask you! Next time I come across her, I'll turn round and walk the other way.'

Cooled off and calmer, he strode without effort along the *quais* as far as the Place de l'Alma, and from there took a taxi back to the Avenue Henri-Martin. The eastern sky was already burnished with dull copper-coloured tints, which seemed rather to betoken the setting of some planet than the dawn of a summer day. No clouds streaked the vault of the heavens, but a haze of particles hung heavy and motionless over Paris, and would presently flare up and smoulder with the sombre glow of red-hot metal. As dawn breaks, the dog-days drain great cities and their suburbs of the moist pinks, floral mauves, and dewy blues that suffuse the sky above open country where plant life flourishes in profusion.

Nothing was stirring in the house when Chéri came to turn the tiny key in the lock. The flagged hall still smelt of the previous evening's dinner, and the cut branches of syringa, arranged by the armful in white vases tall enough to hide a man, filled the air with unbreathable poison. A stray grey cat slipped past him, stopped dead in the middle of the passage, and coldly inspected the intruder.

'Come here, little clerk of the Courts,' Chéri called in a low voice. The cat glared at him almost insultingly and did not budge. Chéri remembered that no animal – no dog, horse, or cat – had ever shown him any signs of affection. He could hear, across a span of fifteen years, Aldonza's raucous voice prophesying: 'A curse lies on those from whom animals turn away.' But when the cat, now wide awake, began to play with a small green chestnut, bowling it along with its front paw, Chéri smiled and went on up to his room.

He found it as dark and blue as a stage night. The dawn penetrated no further than the balcony, bedecked with well trained roses and pelargoniums fastened with raffia. Edmée was asleep, her bare arms and toes peeping out from under a light blanket. She was lying on her side, her head inclined, one finger hooked through her pearls. In the half-light she seemed to be immersed in thought rather than sleep. Her wavy hair strayed over her cheek, and Chéri could hear no sound of her breathing.

'She's enjoying a peaceful sleep,' thought Chéri. 'She's dreaming of Doctor Arnaud, or the Legion of Honour, or Royal Dutch shares. She's pretty. How pretty she is! ... "Don't you worry, only another two or three hours, and you'll go to find your Doctor Arnaud. That's not so bad, is it? You'll meet again in the Avenue de l'Italia, in your beloved joint with its stink of carbolic. You'll answer 'Yes, Doctor; No, Doctor,' like a good little girl. You'll both of you put on really serious expressions; you'll jiggle with thermometers – ninety-nine point six, a hundred and two point four

– and he'll take your small carbolicky paw in his great coal-tarry mitt. You're lucky, my girl, to have a romance in your life! Don't worry. I shan't deprive you of it. ..." I wouldn't mind, myself. ...'

All of a sudden Edmée woke up with such a start that Chéri caught his breath, as though rudely interrupted in the middle of a sentence.

'It's you! It's you! Why, it *is* you after all.'

'If you were expecting someone else, I offer my apologies,' said Chéri, smiling at her.

'That's very clever. ...' She sat up in bed and tossed back her hair. 'What time is it? Are you getting up? Oh no, I see you've not been to bed yet. ... You've just come in. ... Oh, Fred! What have you been up to this time?'

'"This time" is a compliment. ... If you only knew what I've been doing. ...'

She was no longer at the stage where, hands over her ears, she besought him, 'No, no! say nothing! Don't tell me!' But, faster than his wife, Chéri was leaving behind that childishly malicious period when, amidst floods of tears and stormy scenes which ended by her throwing herself into his arms in the early hours of the morning, he would draw her down with him into the deep sleep of reconciled antagonists. No more little games of that sort. ... No more betrayals. ... Nothing, now, but this enforced and unavowable chastity.

He chucked his dusty shoes to the other end of the room, and sat down on the soft lace-frilled sheets, offering his wife a pallid face accustomed to dissemble everything except his will to dissemble. 'Smell me!' he said. 'Come on! I've been drinking whisky.'

She brought her charming mouth to his, putting a hand on her husband's shoulder. 'Whisky ...' she repeated wonderingly. 'Whisky ... why?'

A less sophisticated woman would have asked 'With whom?' and her cunning did not pass unnoticed. Chéri showed that two could play at that game by answering, 'With an old pal. Do you want to hear the whole truth?'

She smiled, now caught in the dawning light which, with growing boldness, touched the edge of the bed, the looking-glass, a picture-frame, and then the golden scales of a fish swimming round and round in a crystal bowl.

'No, Fred, not the whole truth. Only a half-veiled truth, suitable for the small hours.' At the same time, her thoughts were busy. She was certain – or nearly so – that Chéri had not been drawn away from her either by love or by lust. She let her acquiescent body fall helplessly into his arms, yet he felt on his shoulder a thin, hard hand, unrelaxed in its guarded prudence.

'The truth is', he went on, 'that I don't know her name. But I gave her ... wait a moment ... I gave her eighty-three francs.'

'Just like that, all at once! The first time you met her? It's princely!'

She pretended to yawn, and slipped softly back into the depths of the bed, as though not expecting an answer. He gave her a moment's pity; then a brilliant horizontal ray brought into sharper relief the almost naked body lying beside him, and his pity vanished.

'She's ... she has kept her good looks. It's not fair.'

She lay back, her lips parted, looking at him through half-closed eyes. He saw a gleam of the candid, calculating, scarcely feminine expression that a woman bestows on the man who is going to pleasure her, and it shocked his unavowable chastity. From his superior position he returned this look with another – the uncommunicative, enigmatic look of the man who prefers to abstain. Not wishing to move away, he simply looked towards the golden daylight, the freshness of the watered garden, and the blackbirds, weaving liquid sequences of sound round the dry incessant chirps of the sparrows. Edmée could see signs of emaciation and prolonged fatigue on his features. His cheeks were blue with a day's growth of beard. She noticed that his fine hands were not clean, that his finger-nails had not been near soap and water since the previous evening, and that the dark lines which accentuated the hollows under his eyes were now spreading, in the shape of crow's feet, towards his nose. This handsome young man – she decided – without collar or shoes, looked ravaged, as if he had had to spend a night in prison. Without losing his looks, he had shrunk in accordance with some mysterious scaling down, and this enabled her to regain the upper hand. She no longer invited him to join her, sat up in bed, and put a hand on his forehead.

'Ill?'

Slowly he let his attention wander back from the garden to his wife.

'What? ... No, no, nothing's wrong with me, except I'm sleepy. So sleepy that I can hardly bring myself to go to bed – if you know what I mean. ...'

He smiled, showing dry gums and lips colourless on the insides. But, above all, this smile betrayed a sadness that sought no remedy, modest as a poor man's suffering. Edmée was on the point of questioning him categorically, but then thought better of it.

'Get into bed,' she ordered, making room for him.

'Bed? It's water I need. I feel so filthy, it just isn't true.'

He just had the strength to lift up a water-bottle, take a gulp from the neck, then throw off his coat, before he fell back like a log on the bed, and lay there without moving again, drained by sleep.

For some little time Edmée gazed at the half-stripped stranger lying like a drugged man beside her. Her watchful eye wandered from bluish lips to hollowed eyes, from outflung hand to forehead sealed upon a single secret. She summoned her self-control and composed her features, as though afraid the sleeper might take her by surprise. She got out of bed softly, and, before shutting out the dazzling sunlight, drew a silk counterpane to hide the outstretched untidy body looking like a burglar who had been knocked out. She arranged this so as to give the beautiful rigid features their full splendour, carefully pulling it down over the drooping hand with a slight qualm of pious disgust, as though hiding a weapon that perhaps had killed.

He never twitched a muscle – having retired for a few moments within an impregnable fastness. In any case, Edmée's hospital training had given her fingers a professional touch, which, if not exactly gentle, was competent to go straight to the required spot without touching or in any way affecting the surrounding area. She did not get back into bed; but, sitting half-naked, enjoyed the unexpected freshness of the hour when the sun rouses the winds. The long curtains stirred, as if breathing and, dependent on the breeze, stippled Chéri's sleep with fitful flecks of dark blue.

As she gazed at him, Edmée was not thinking of the wounded, or of the dead, whose peasant hands she had joined together upon coarse cotton sheets. No invalid in the grip of a nightmare, not one among the dead, had ever resembled Chéri: sleep, silence, and repose made him magnificently inhuman.

Extreme beauty arouses no sympathy. It is not the prerogative of any one country. Time's finger had touched Chéri only to make him more austere. The mind – whose task it is to curb the splendour of mankind while degrading it piecemeal – respected Chéri as an admirable temple dedicated to instinct. What could avail the Machiavellian deceit, the ardour, and the cunning self-sacrifice imposed by love, against this inviolable standard-bearer of light and his untutored majesty?

Patient and, on occasion, subtle as she was, it never occurred to Edmée that the feminine appetite for possession tends to emasculate every living conquest, and can reduce a magnificent but inferior male to the status of a courtesan. Her lower-middle-class wisdom made her determined not to relinquish the gains – money, ease, domestic tyranny, marriage – acquired in so few years and rendered doubly attractive by the war.

She gazed at the limp, worn-out, almost empty-looking body. 'That's Chéri,' she said to herself; 'yes, that's Chéri all right ... That's how small a thing he is!' She shrugged a shoulder and added: 'That's what he's reduced to, this wonderful Chéri of theirs ...' doing her best to induce contempt for the man lying thus supine. She called up memories of rapturous nights, of languid early mornings bathed in sunlight and pleasure, and, as a result – since he had progressively grown to disdain her – she saw fit to pay but coldly vindictive homage to this body so sumptuously laid out under the pall of flowered silk and the refreshing wing of the curtains. She put one hand on the small, pointed breast set low on her slender body, and squeezed it like a pulpy fruit, as if calling this most tempting allurement of her young body to witness the injustice of his desertion. 'What Chéri himself needs is doubtless something else. What he needs is ...'

But vain were her attempts to put her scorn into words. Even a woman loses the desire and the ability to despise a man who suffers in silence and alone.

All of a sudden, Edmée felt satiated with the spectacle: the shadows thrown by the curtains, the pallor of the sleeper, and the white bed helped to invest it with the romantic colouring of death and the nether world. She jumped to her feet, strong and ready to face this world, but determined to avoid any emotional attack upon the traitor lying on the disordered bed, the absentee seeking refuge in sleep, silent, ailing, and repulsive. She was neither irritated nor unhappy. Her heart would beat more feverishly in her breast, the blood mount more quickly to her pearl-pale cheeks, only at the thought of the healthy red-haired man whom she called 'dear master' or 'chief' in tones of serious playfulness. Arnaud's thick gentle hands; his laugh; the points of light that sunshine or the lamp in the operating theatre caused to twinkle on his red moustache; his very coat – the white surgery coat he wore and even took off in the hospital, just like an intimate garment that never passes beyond the bedroom door. ... Edmée sprang up as though for a dance.

'That, oh yes, *that's* my life!' She gave a toss of the head that sent her hair flying out like a horse's mane, and went into the bathroom without turning round.

UNIMAGINATIVE in style, and in its very ordinary proportions, the dining-room made no pretence to luxury except in the panels of yellow stuff starred with purple and green. The grey and white stucco of the surrounding walls deflected too much light on the guests, deprived already of all shade by the merciless glare of the top lighting.

A galaxy of crystal sequins shimmered with every movement of Edmée's dress. For the family dinner, Madame Peloux was still wearing her tailor-made with leather buttons, and Camille de La Berche her nurse's veil, under the cowl of which she bore a striking resemblance to Dante, only far hairier. Because it was so hot, the women spoke little: so did Chéri, because it was his habit. A warm bath followed by a cold shower had triumphed over his fatigue; but the powerful light, ricocheting upon his cheeks, accentuated their cavities, and he kept his eyes lowered, to allow the shadow from his eyebrows to fall directly over the lids.

'Tonight, Chéri doesn't look a day over sixteen,' boomed the deep bass of the Baroness out of the blue.

No one took up her remark, and Chéri acknowledged it with a slight bow.

'Not for a long time', the Baroness continued, 'have I seen the oval of his face so slender.'

Edmée frowned imperceptibly. 'I have. During the war, of course.'

'That's true, that's true,' piped Charlotte Peloux in shrill agreement. 'Heavens! how worn out he looked in 1916, at Vésoul! Edmée, my dear child,' she went on in the same breath, 'I've seen you-know-who today, and *everything* is going along very nicely. ...'

Edmée blushed in a docile, unbecoming manner, and Chéri raised his eyes. 'You've seen who? And what's going along nicely?'

'Trousellier's pension – my little soldier who's had his right arm off. He left the Hospital on June the twentieth. Your mother's taking up his case at the War Office.'

She had not hesitated for words, and she let her calm golden gaze rest on Chéri: yet he knew she was lying.

'It's a question of whether he'll get his red riband. After all, poor boy, it's certainly his turn. ...'

She was lying to him in front of two friends who knew that she was lying. 'Why don't I pick up the water-bottle and crash it down in the middle of them?' But he made no movement. What strength of feeling would have given him the impetus to brace his body and direct his hand?

'Abzac is leaving us in a week's time,' began Madame de La Berche.

'That's not certain,' Edmée took her up with an air of knowing better. 'Doctor Arnaud isn't at all satisfied that he should be allowed to go off like that on his new leg. You can just see the man, liable to do any sort of silly thing, and always with the possibility of gangrene. Doctor Arnaud knows only too well that it was exactly that sort of thing, all through the war. ...'

Chéri looked at her, and she stopped abruptly in the middle of her pointless sentence. She was fanning herself with a rose on a leafy stalk. She waved away a dish which she was offered, and put her elbows on the table. In her white dress and bare shoulders, even when sitting still, she was not exempt from a secret contentment, a self-satisfaction, which revealed her true nature. Something outrageous radiated from her soft outlines. Some tell-tale glow betrayed the woman bent on 'arriving', who up till the present had met only with success.

'Edmée', Chéri concluded, 'is a woman who should never grow older than twenty. How like her mother she's getting!'

The next moment the resemblance had vanished. Nothing obvious about Edmée recalled Marie-Laure: only in one respect did her daughter exhibit something of the poisonous, pink and white, impudent beauty exploited by the red-haired Marie-Laure to ensnare her victims during her palmy days – and that was in her shamelessness. Careful as she was not to shock anyone, those who still retained their native shrewdness, by instinct or from lack of education, were shocked by her all the same, as if by a second-rate race-horse, or a jewel that looked too new. The servants, as well as Chéri, were frightened of something in Edmée, whom they guessed to be more vulgar than themselves.

Authorized by Edmée, who was lighting a cigarette, the Baroness de La Berche slowly grilled the tip of her cigar before inhaling the first rapturous puff. Her white Red Cross veil fell over her manly shoulders and she looked like one of those grave-faced men who, at Christmas parties, adorn their heads with tissue-paper Phrygian caps, programme-sellers' kerchiefs, or shakos. Charlotte undid the plaited leather buttons of her jacket and drew towards her a box of Abdullas; while the butler, mindful of the customs of the house, pushed within easy reach of Chéri a small conjuror's table on wheels – full of secret drawers, sliding double-bottomed compartments, and liqueurs in silver phials. Then he left the room; and there was no longer against the yellow panels the tall silhouette of an elderly Italian with a face carved out of box-wood, and crowned with white hair.

'Old Giacomo really does look an aristocrat,' said the Baroness de La Berche, 'and I know what I'm talking about.'

Madame Peloux shrugged her shoulders, a movement that had long since ceased to lift her breasts. Her white silk blouse with a jabot sagged under the weight of her bosom, and her short, dyed, but still abundant hair glowed a livid red above large disastrous eyes and high forehead, suggesting a leader of the French Revolution.

'He's got the distinguished looks of all elderly Italians with white hair. They're all Papal Chamberlains, by the look of them, and they can write out the menu for you in Latin; but you've only to open a door and you'll find them raping a little girl of seven.'

Chéri welcomed this outburst of virulence as a timely shower. His mother's malice had parted the clouds again, bringing back an atmosphere in which he could breathe. Not so long ago he had begun to enjoy discovering traces of the old Charlotte, who, from the safety of her balcony, would refer to a pretty woman passing below as 'a tuppenny-ha'penny tart', and who, to Chéri's 'Do you know her, then?' would reply, 'No! Whatever next! Do you expect me to know that slut?' Only recently had he begun to take a confused pleasure in Charlotte's superior vitality, and, confusedly, he now preferred her to the other two creatures present; but he was unaware that this preference, this partiality, could perhaps be termed filial affection. He laughed, and applauded Madame Peloux for still being

– and quite startlingly so – the woman he had known, detested, feared, and insulted. For an instant, Madame Peloux took on her authentic character in her son's eyes; that is to say, he estimated her at her proper value, a woman high-spirited, all-consuming, calculating, and at the same time rash, like a high financier; a woman capable of taking a humorist's delight in spiteful cruelty. 'She's a scourge, certainly,' he said to himself, 'and no more. A scourge, but not a stranger.' Looking at the way the points of her hair impinged upon her Jacobin forehead, he recognized a similarity to the blue-black jutting points on his own forehead, which emphasized the whiteness of his skin and the blackbird sheen of his hair.

'She's my mother all right,' he thought. 'No one's ever told me I'm like her, but I am.' The 'stranger' was sitting opposite, glimmering with the milky, veiled brilliance of a pearl. Chéri heard the name of the Duchess of Camastra thrown out by the deep voice of the Baroness, and on the stranger's face he saw a fleeting rapacity flicker and die like the serpent of flame that suddenly flares up along a burnt vine-twig before it is consumed among the embers. But she did not open her mouth, and took no part in the volley of military curses which the Baroness was firing at a hospital rival.

'They're properly in the soup, it appears, over some new-fangled injection or other. Two men died within two days of being given the needle. That needs some explaining!' said Madame de La Berche with a hearty laugh.

'You've got it wrong,' corrected Edmée dryly. 'That's an old story of Janson-de-Sailly resuscitated.'

'No smoke without fire,' sighed Charlotte charitably. 'Chéri, are you sleepy?'

He was dropping with fatigue, but he admired the powers of resistance of these three women: neither hard work, the Parisian summer, nor perpetual movement and jabber could put them out of action.

'The heat,' he murmured laconically. He caught Edmée's eye, but she made no comment and refrained from contradicting him.

'Pooh, pooh, pooh,' chanted Charlotte. 'The heat! But, of course. ... Pooh, pooh, pooh.'

Her eyes, which remained fixed on Chéri's, overflowed with

blackmailing tenderness and complicity. As usual, she knew everything there was to be known: backstairs gossip, concierges' chatter. Perhaps Léa herself, for the pleasure of a feminine fib, of winning one last trick, had told Charlotte. The Baroness de La Berche emitted a little neigh, and the shadow of her large clerical nose covered the lower part of her face.

'God in Heaven!' swore Chéri.

His chair fell to the floor behind him, and Edmée, alert and on the watch, promptly jumped to her feet. She showed not the slightest astonishment. Charlotte Peloux and the Baroness de La Berche at once put themselves on the defensive, but in the old-fashioned way – hands clutching skirts, ready to gather them up and fly. Chéri, leaning forward with his fists on the table, was panting and turning his head to right and left, like a wild animal caught in a net.

'You, to start with, you ...' he stammered. He pointed at Charlotte; used as she was to such scenes, she was galvanized by this filial threat in the presence of witnesses.

'What? What? What?' she barked in sharp little yelps. 'You dare to insult me? a little whippersnapper like you, a wretched little whippersnapper who, were I to open my mouth ...'

The wine-glasses quivered at the sound of her piercing voice, but her words were cut short by a shriller voice: 'Leave him alone!'

After three such abrupt explosions the silence seemed deafening, and Chéri, his physical dignity restored, shook himself, and a smile spread over his green face.

'I beg your pardon, Madame Peloux,' he said mischievously.

She was already conferring blessings on him with eye and hand, like a champion in the ring, pacified at the end of a round.

'You're hot-blooded and no mistake!'

'He's a soldier all right,' said the Baroness, as she shook hands with Edmée. 'I must say goodbye, Chéri; they'll be missing me in my dug-out.'

She refused a lift in Charlotte's motor, and insisted on going home on foot. The tall figure, the white nurse's veil, and the glow of her cigar would strike terror at night into the heart of the fiercest footpad. Edmée accompanied the two old women as far as the front door, an exceptional act of courtesy, which allowed Chéri time to draw what conclusions he could from his wife's wary action and her diplomatic peacemaking.

He drank a glass of cold water very slowly, as he stood beneath the cataract of light, thinking the matter over and savouring his terrible loneliness.

'She defended me,' he kept repeating to himself. 'She defended me with no love in her heart. She protected me as she protects the garden against blackbirds, her store of sugar against thieving nurses, or her cellar against the footmen. Little doubt she knows that I went to the Rue Raynouard, and came back here, never to go there again. She's not said a word about it to me, in any case – perhaps because she doesn't care. She protected me, because it wouldn't have done for my mother to talk. She defended me with no love in her heart.'

He heard Edmée's voice in the garden. She was testing his mood from afar. 'You don't feel ill, Fred, do you? Would you like to go straight to bed?'

She put her head through the half-open door, and he laughed bitterly to himself: 'How cautious she's being.'

She saw his smile and grew bolder. 'Come along, Fred. I believe I'm just as tired as you, or I wouldn't have let myself go just now. I've been apologizing to your mother.'

She switched off some of the cruel light, and gathered the roses from the table-cloth to put them into water. Her body, her hands, her head bending over the roses and set off by a haze of fair hair from which the heat had taken most of the crimp – everything about her might have charmed a man.

'I said *a man* – I didn't say *any man*,' Léa's insidious voice kept ringing in Chéri's ears.

'I can behave as I like to her,' he thought, as he followed Edmée with his eyes. 'She'll never complain, she'll never divorce me; I've nothing to fear from her, not even love. I should be happy enough, if I chose.'

But, at the same time, he recoiled with unspeakable repugnance from the idea of the two of them living together in a home where love no longer held sway. His childhood as a bastard, his long adolescence as a ward, had taught him that his world, though people thought of it as reckless, was governed by a code almost as narrow-minded as middle-class prejudice. In it, Chéri had learned that love is a question of money, infidelity, betrayals, and cowardly resignation. But now he was well on the way to forgetting the rules he had been taught, and to be repelled by acts of silent condescension.

He therefore ignored the gentle hand on his sleeve. And, as he walked with Edmée towards the room whence would issue no sound of endearment or reproach, he was overcome with shame, and blushed at the horror of their unspoken agreement.

H E found himself out of doors, dressed for the street and hardly conscious of having put on his soft hat and light raincoat. Behind him lay the drawing-room, misty with tobacco smoke; the overpowering scent of women and flowers; the cyanide smell of cherry brandy. There he had left Edmée, Doctor Arnaud, Filipesco, Atkins, and the two Kelekian girls, well-connected young women who, having done a little mild lorry-driving during the war, had no use now for anything but cigars, motors, and their garage-hand friends. He had left Desmond sitting between a real estate merchant and an Under-Secretary in the Ministry of Commerce, together with an invalided poet and Charlotte Peloux. Also a fashionable young married couple, who had obviously been put wise. Throughout dinner they had looked greedy but prudish, with a knowing expression and a simple-minded eagerness to be shocked – as though expecting Chéri to dance stark naked, or Charlotte and the Under-Secretary to make violent love to one another in the middle of the carpet.

Chéri had made off, aware that his behaviour had been stoical, with no other lapse than a sudden loss of interest in the present: an awkward thing to lose in the middle of a meal. Even so, his trance could have lasted little more than a moment, had been instantaneous, like a dream. But now he was putting a distance between himself and the strangers who thronged his house, and the sound of his footfall on the sand was as light as the soft padding of an animal. His light silver-grey coat shaded into the mist that had fallen over the Bois; and a few nocturnal loiterers must have envied a young man who was in such a hurry to go nowhere in particular.

He was haunted by the vision of his crowded house. He could still hear the sound of voices, and carried with him the memory of faces, of smiles, and especially of the shape of mouths. An elderly man had talked about the war; a woman about politics. He remembered, too, the new understanding between Desmond and Edmée, and the interest his wife had taken in some building scheme. 'Desmond! ... Just the husband for my wife!' And then, dancing ... the strange effect of the tango on Charlotte Peloux. Chéri quickened his step.

The night was filled with the damp mist of a too early autumn and the full moon was shrouded. A great milky halo, ringed with a pallid iridescence, had replaced the planet, and was sometimes itself hidden by fitful puffs of scudding cloud. The smell of September was already in the leaves that had fallen during the dog days.

'How mild it is,' Chéri thought.

He rested his weary limbs on a bench, but not for long. He was rejoined by an invisible companion, to whom he refused his seat on the bench – a woman with grey hair, wearing a long coat, who poured forth a relentless gaiety. Chéri turned his head towards the gardens of La Muette, as though he could hear, even at that distance, the cymbals of the jazz-band.

The time had not yet come for him to go back to the blue room, where perhaps the two society girls were still smoking good cigars, as they sat side-saddle on the blue velvet of the bed, keeping the real estate merchant amused with mess-room tales.

'Oh! for a nice hotel bedroom, a jolly pink room, very ordinary and very pink …' But would it not lose its very ordinariness the moment the light was turned out and total darkness gave the right of entry – a ponderous, mocking entry – to a figure with vigorous grey hair, dressed in a long, nondescript coat? He smiled at the intruder, for he was past the stage of fear. 'There, or in any other place, *she* will be just as faithful. But I simply can't go on living with those people.'

Day by day, hour by hour, he was becoming more scornful, more exacting. Already he was severely critical of the Agony Column heroes, and young war widows who clamoured for new husbands, like the parched for cold water. His uncompromising intolerance extended to the world of finance, without his realizing how grave was the change. 'That Company for transporting raw hides they talked about at dinner. … How disgusting it was! And they don't mind discussing it at the top of their voices. …' But nothing in the world would have induced him to protest, to reveal that he was fast becoming a man utterly out of sympathy with his surroundings. Prudently, he kept quiet about that, as about everything else. When he had taken Charlotte Peloux to task for having disposed of several tons of sugar in rather a dubious fashion, had she not reminded him – and in no uncertain terms – of the time when he had shouted, without a trace of embarrassment, 'Hand over five louis, Léa, so that I can go and buy some cigarettes'?

'Ah!' he sighed, 'they'll never understand anything, these women. It wasn't at all the same thing.'

Thus he let his thoughts run on, as he stood, bareheaded, his hair glistening, barely distinguishable in the mist. The shadowy form of a female passed close beside him, running. The rhythm of her steps and the crunch as each foot bit into the gravel betrayed anxiety and haste. Then the shadowy woman fell into the arms of a shadowy man who came to meet her, and down they fell together, breast to breast, as though struck by the same bullet.

'Those two are trying to hide,' Chéri thought. 'They're deceiving someone somewhere. The whole world's busy deceiving and being deceived. But I ...' He did not finish the sentence, but a repugnance made him jump to his feet, an action that meant, 'But I am chaste.' A faint ray of light, flickering uncertainly over stagnant, hitherto unfeeling regions of his inmost being, was enough to suggest that chastity and loneliness are one and the same misfortune.

As night advanced, he began to feel the cold. From his prolonged, aimless vigils, he had learned that, at night, tastes, smells, and temperatures vary according to the hour, and that midnight is warm in comparison with the hour which immediately precedes the dawn.

'The winter will soon be on us,' he thought, as he lengthened his stride, 'and none too soon, putting an end to this interminable summer. Next winter, I should like ... let me see ... next winter ...' His attempts at anticipation collapsed almost at once; and he came to a halt, head lowered, like a horse at the prospect of a long steep climb ahead.

'Next winter, there'll still be my wife, my mother, old gammer La Berche, Thingummy, What's-his-name, and the rest of them. There'll be the same old gang. ... And for me there'll never again be ...'

84

He paused once more, to watch a procession of low clouds advancing over the Bois, clouds of an indescribable pink, set upon by a gusty wind which buried its fingers in their misty tresses, twisting and dragging them across the lawns of heaven, to carry them off to the moon. Chéri gazed with eyes well used to the translucent magic of the night, which those who sleep regard as pitch-dark.

The apparition of the large, flat, half-veiled moon among the scurrying vaporous clouds, which she seemed to be pursuing and tearing asunder, did not divert him from working out an arithmetical fantasy: he was computing – in years, months, hours, and days – the amount of precious time that had been lost to him for ever.

'Had I never let her go when I went to see her again that day before the war – then it would have meant three or four years to the good; hundreds and hundreds of days and nights gained and garnered for love.' He did not fight shy of so big a word.

'Hundreds of days – a lifetime – life itself. Life as it was in the old days, life with my "worst enemy", as she used to call herself. My worst enemy! who forgave me all, and never let me off a single thing.' He seized hold of his past, to squeeze out every remaining drop upon his empty, arid present; bringing back to life, and inventing where necessary, the princely days of his youth, his adolescence shaped and guided by a woman's strong capable hands – loving hands, ever ready to chastise. A prolonged, sheltered, oriental adolescence, in which the pleasures of the flesh had their passing place, like silent pauses in a song. A life of luxury, passing whims, childish cruelty, with fidelity a yet unspoken word.

He threw back his head to look up at the nacreous halo which irradiated the whole sky, and he gave a low cry, 'It's all gone to hell! I'm thirty years old!'

He hurried on his way back home, heaping curses on himself to the rhythm of his quickened steps. 'Fool! The tragedy is not her age, but mine. Everything may be over for her, but, for me ...'

He let himself in without making a sound, to find the house in silence at last; to be nauseated by the lingering stale smell of those who had dined, wined, and danced there. In the looking-glass fitted to the door in the hall he met face to face the young man who had grown so thin, whose cheeks had hardened, whose sad beautifully moulded upper lip was unshaven and blue, whose large eyes were reticent and tragic. The young man, in effect, who had ceased, inexplicably, to be twenty-four years old.

'For me,' Chéri completed his thought, 'I really do believe that the last word has been said.'

'WHAT I need is somewhere quiet, you understand. ... Any little place would do. ... A bachelor flat, a room, a corner. ...'

'I wasn't born yesterday,' said the Pal reproachfully.

She raised disconsolate eyes towards the festoons on the ceiling: 'A little love, of course, of course, a little kiss – something to warm a poor lonely heart. ... You bet I understand! Any special fancy?'

Chéri frowned. 'Fancy? For whom?'

'You don't understand, my pretty. ... Fancy for any particular district?'

'Ah! ... No, nothing special. Just a quiet corner.'

The Pal nodded her large head in collusion. 'I see, I see. Something after my style – like my flat. You know where I rest my bones?'

'Yes.'

'No, you don't know at all. I was certain you wouldn't write it down. Two hundred and fourteen Rue de Villiers. It's not big, and it's not beautiful. But you don't want the sort of place where the whole street knows your business.'

'No.'

'I got mine, of course, through a little deal with my landlady. A jewel of a woman, by the way, married, or as good as. Periwinkle blue eyes, and a head like a bird; but she bears the mark of Fate on her forehead, and I already know from her cards that she can't say no to anything, and that –'

'Yes, yes. You were saying just now that you knew of a flat ...'

'Yes, but not good enough for you.'

'You don't think so?'

'Not for you ... not for the two of you!'

The Pal hid a suggestive smile in her whisky, and Chéri turned from its smell – like wet harness. He put up with her quips about his imaginary conquests, for he saw, round her scraggy neck, a string of large faked pearls which he thought he recognized. Every visual reminder of his past halted him on his downward path, and, during such respites, he felt at peace.

87

'Ah!' sighed the Pal. 'How I'd love to catch a glimpse of her! What a pair! ... I don't know her, of course, but I can just see you two together! ... Of course you'll provide everything yourself?'

'For whom?'

'Why, the furniture in your love-nest, of course!'

He looked at the Pal in bewilderment. Furniture ... What furniture? He had been thinking only of one thing: a refuge of his own, with a door that opened and closed for him and no one else, safe from Edmée, Charlotte, all of them. ...

'Will you furnish it in period or in modern style? La belle Serrano arranged her entire ground floor with nothing but Spanish shawls, but that was a bit eccentric. You're old enough, of course, to know your own mind. ...'

He hardly heard her, far away in his dreams of a future home that would be secret, small, warm, and dark. At the same time, he was drinking red-currant syrup, like any young 'miss', in the red-and-gold, out-of-date, unchanging bar, just as it used to be when, a small boy, Chéri had come there to sip his first fizzy drink through a straw. ... Even the barman himself had not changed, and if the woman sitting opposite Chéri was now a withered specimen, at least he had never known her beautiful, or young.

'They all change, the whole of that set – my mother, my wife, all the people they see – and they live for change. My mother may change into a banker, Edmée into a town councillor. But I ...'

In imagination, he quickly returned to that refuge, existing at some unknown point in space, but secret, small, warm, and ...

'Mine's done up in Algerian style,' the Pal persisted. 'It's no longer in the fashion, but I don't mind – especially as the furniture is hired. You'll be sure to recognize many of the photos I've put up: and then there's the portrait of La Loupiote. ... Come and have a look at it. Please do.'

'I'd like to. Let's go!'

On the threshold he hailed a taxi.

'But d'you never have your motor? Why haven't you got your motor? It's really quite extraordinary how people with motors never have their motor!'

She gathered up her faded black skirts, caught the string of her lorgnette in the clasp of her bag, dropped a glove, and submitted to the stares of the passers-by with the lack of embarrassment of a Negro. Chéri, standing at her side, received several insulting smiles and the admiring condolences of a young woman, who called out: 'Lord, what a waste of good material!'

In the taxi, patiently and half asleep, he endured the old thing's tattle. And then some of her stories were soothing: the one about the ridiculous little dog which had held up the return from the races in 1897, and then Mère La Berche eloping with a young bride on the day of her wedding in 1893.

'That's it over there. This door's stuck, Chéri, I can't get out. I warn you, there's not much light in the passage, nor, for that matter, is there much out here. ... It's only a ground-floor flat, when all's said and done! ... Wait where you are a second.'

He waited, standing in the semi-darkness. He heard the jingle of keys, the wheezy old creature's gasps for breath, and then her fussy servant's voice, 'I'm lighting up. ... Then you'll find yourself in a familiar landscape. I've got electricity, of course. ... There, let me introduce you to my little morning-room, which is also my large drawing-room!'

He went in, and, from kindness – hardly bothering to glance at it – praised the room; it had a low ceiling and reddish walls, kippered by the smoke of innumerable cigars and cigarettes. Instinctively, he looked all round for the window, barricaded by shutters and curtains.

'You can't see in here? You're not an old night-bird like your Pal. Wait, I'll switch on the top light.'

'Don't bother. ... I'll just come in and –' He broke off, staring at the most brightly lit wall, covered with small frames and photographs pinned through the four corners. The Pal began to laugh.

'What did I say about a familiar landscape! I was quite sure you'd enjoy looking at them. You haven't got that one, have you?'

'That one' was a very large photographic portrait-study, touched up with water-colours now quite faded. Blue eyes, a laughing mouth, a chignon of fair hair, and a look of calm yet exultant triumph. ... High-breasted – in a First Empire corselet, legs showing through gauze skirts, legs that never finished, rounded out at the thigh, slender at the knee, legs that ... And a fetching hat, a hat that turned up on one side only, trimmed like a single sail to the wind.

'She never gave you that one, not that one, I bet! It makes her a goddess, a fairy walking on clouds! And yet it's absolutely her, of course. This big photo is the loveliest, to my way of thinking, but I'm still every bit as fond of the others. Here, for instance, look at this little one here – much more recent, of course – isn't it a sight for sore eyes?'

A snapshot, clinging to the wall with the help of a rusty pin, showed a woman standing in the shade against a sunlit garden.

'It's the navy-blue dress and the hat with the seagulls,' Chéri said to himself.

'I'm all for flattering portraits, myself,' the Pal went on. 'A portrait like this one. Come now – you must confess – isn't it enough to make you join your hands and believe in God?'

A degraded and smarmy art, to lend glamour to the 'portrait photograph', had lengthened the neck line and modified those around the sitter's mouth. But the nose, just sufficiently aquiline, the delicious nose with its ravishing nostrils, and the chaste little dimple, the velvety cleft that indented the upper lip under the nose – these were untouched, authentic, respected by even the photographer.

'Would you believe it? She wanted to burn the lot, pretending that nobody today is the least interested in what she used to be like. My blood boiled, I shrieked like a soul in torment, and she gave me the whole collection the very same day that she made me a present of the bag with her monogram. ...'

'Who's this fellow with her ... here ... in this one underneath?'

'What were you saying? What's that? Wait till I take off my hat.'

'I'm asking you who this is – this fellow – here. Get a move on, can't you?'

'Heavens, don't bustle me about so. ... That? It's Bacciocchi, come! Naturally, you can hardly be expected to recognize him, he dates from two turns before you.'

'Two what?'

'After Bacciocchi, she had Septfons – and yet no – wait ... Septfons was earlier than that. ... Septfons, Bacciocchi, Spéleïeff, and you.

Oh! do look at those check trousers! ... How ridiculous men's fashions used to be!'

'And that photo over there; when was that taken?'

He drew back a step, for at his elbow the Pal's head was craning forward, and its magpie's nest of felted hair smelt like a wig.

'That? That's her costume for Auteuil in ... in 1888, or '89. Yes, the year of the Exhibition. In front of that one, dear boy, you should raise your hat. They don't turn out beauties like that any more.'

'Pooh! ... I don't think it so stunning.'

The Pal folded her hands. Hatless, she looked older, and her high forehead was a buttery yellow under hair dyed greenish black.

'Not so stunning! That waist you could encircle with your ten fingers! That lily neck! And be good enough to let your eyes rest on that dress! All in frilled sky-blue chiffon, dear boy, and looped up with little pink moss-roses sewn on to the frills, and the hat to match! And the little bag to match as well – we called them alms-bags at that time. Oh! the beauty she was then! There's been nothing since to compare with her first appearances: she was the dawn, the very sun of love.'

'First appearances where?'

She gave Chéri a gentle dig in the ribs. 'Get along with you. ... How you make me laugh! Ah! the trials of life must melt into thin air when you're about the house!' '

His rigid features passed unobserved. He was still facing the wall, seemingly riveted by several Léas – one smelling an artificial rose, another bending over a book with medieval hasps, her swan neck rising from a pleatless collar, a white and rounded neck like the bole of a birch-tree.

'Well, I must be going,' he said, like Valérie Cheniaguine.

'What d'you mean – you must be going? What about my dining-room? And my bedroom? just glance at them, my pretty! Take a note of them for your little love-nest.'

'Ah! yes. ... Listen; not today, because ...' He glanced distrust-fully towards the rampart of portraits, and lowered his voice. 'I've an appointment. But I'll come back ... tomorrow. Probably to-morrow, before dinner.'

'Good. Then I can go ahead?'

'Go ahead?'

'With the flat.'

'Yes, that's right. See about it. And thanks.'

'I really begin to wonder what the world's coming to. ... Young or old – it's hard to tell which are the most disgusting. ... Two "turns" before me! ... and "the first appearances," said the old spider, "the dazzling first appearances." ... And all quite openly. No, really, what a world!'

He found that he had been keeping up the pace of a professional walker in training, and that he was out of breath. And all the more because the distant storm – which would not burst over Paris – had walled off what breeze there was behind a violet bastion, now towering straight up against the sky. Alongside the fortifications of the Boulevard Berthier, under trees stripped bare by the summer drought, a sparse crowd of Parisians in rope-soled sandals and a few half-naked children in red jerseys seemed to be waiting for a tidal wave to come rolling up from Levallois-Perret. Chéri sat down on a bench, forgetting that his strength was apt to play him tricks. He was unaware that his strength was being sapped in some mysterious manner ever since he had started to fritter it away on night vigils, and had neglected to exercise or nourish his body.

'"Two turns!" Really! Two turns before me! And after me, how many? Add the whole lot together, myself included, and how many turns d'you get?'

Beside a blue-clad, seagull-hatted Léa, he could see a tall, broad Spéleïeff, smiling expansively. He remembered a sad Léa, red-eyed with weeping, stroking his head when he was a small boy and calling him a 'horrid little man in the making'.

'Léa's lover' ... 'Léa's new pet' ... Traditional and meaningless words – as common on everyone's lips as talk about the weather, the latest odds at Auteuil, or the dishonesty of servants. 'Are you coming, kid?' Spéleïeff would say to Chéri. 'We'll go out and have a porto at Armenonville, while we wait for Léa to join us. Nothing would drag her out of bed this morning.'

'She's got a ravishing new little Bacciocchi,' Madame Peloux had informed her son, aged fourteen or fifteen at the time.

But, a bundle of sophistication and innocence, brought up in the midst of love, yet blinded by its proximity, Chéri, at that tender age, had talked love, as children learn a language by ear, picking up words, pleasant or filthy, merely as sounds without meaning. No vivid or voluptuous vision arose behind the shadow of this huge Spéleïeff so recently risen from Léa's bed. And was there really very much difference between this 'ravishing little Bacciocchi' and a 'prize Pekingese'?

No photograph or letter, no story from the only lips that might have told him the truth, had blighted the enclosed Paradise in which Léa and Chéri had dwelt for so many years. Next to nothing in Chéri existed which dated back beyond Léa: why, then, should he bother about a man who, before his day, had brought warmth or sadness or riches to his mistress?

A fair-haired little boy with fat knees came and planted his crossed arms on the bench beside Chéri. They glared at each other with identical expressions of offended reserve, for Chéri treated all children as strangers. For some time this boy let his pale blue eyes rest on Chéri, who watched some sort of indescribable smile, full of scorn, mount up from the small anaemic mouth to the flax-blue pupils of the eyes. Then the child turned away, and, picking up his dirty toys from the dust, began to play at the foot of the bench, blotting Chéri out of existence. Then Chéri got up and walked away.

Half an hour later, he was lying in a warm, scented bath, clouded by some milky bath essence. He lay revelling in its luxury and comfort, in the soft lather of the soap, and in the remote faint sounds about the house, as though they were the rewards of an act of great courage, or else blessings he was tasting for the last time.

His wife came into the room humming, broke off at the sight of him, and narrowly failed to disguise her speechless astonishment at finding Chéri at home and in his bath.

'Am I in your way?' he asked, with no irony.

'Not in the least, Fred.'

She began to take off her day clothes with youthful abandon, with total disregard for modesty or immodesty, and Chéri was amused by her haste to be undressed and in a bath.

'How completely I'd forgotten her,' he thought, as he looked at the odalisque back, supple but well-covered, of the woman bending down to untie her shoelaces.

She did not speak to him, but went about her business like a woman who believes she is safely by herself, and in front of his eyes rose the figure of the child who, not long since, had been playing in the dust at his feet, resolutely ignoring his presence.

'Tell me ...'

Edmée raised a surprised forehead, a soft half-naked body.

'What would you say to our having a child?'

'Fred! ... What are you thinking of?'

It was almost a cry of terror, and already Edmée was clutching a wisp of lawn close to her bosom with one hand, while with the other she groped, fumbling, for the first kimono within reach. Chéri could not hold back his laughter.

'Would you like my revolver? I'm not going to assault you.'

'Why are you laughing?' she asked, almost in a whisper. 'You should never laugh.'

'I seldom laugh. But do tell me ... now that all is quiet and peaceful between us ... do tell me why. Are you really so terrified at the thought that we could have had, could still have, a child?'

'Yes,' she said cruelly, and her unexpected frankness shocked even herself.

She never took her eyes off her husband, lying full-length in a low armchair, and she murmured distinctly enough for him to hear, 'A child ... who'd be sure to take after you. You twice over, you twice over in the single lifetime of one woman? No. ... Oh, no.'

He began a gesture which she misinterpreted.

'No, I beg of you. ... There's nothing more to be said. I won't even discuss it. Let's leave things as they are. We've only to be a little cautious, and go on ... I ask nothing of you ...'

'That suits you?'

Her only answer was to put on a look, insulting in its misery and plaintive helplessness, a seraglio look that well suited her nakedness. Her freshly powdered cheeks, the touch of colour on her youthful lips, the light brown halo round her hazel eyes, the care bestowed on every feature of her face, were in striking contrast to the confusion

94

of her body, bare except for the crumpled silk shift she was clasping to her breasts.

'I can no longer make her happy,' thought Chéri, 'but I can still make her suffer. She is not altogether unfaithful to me. Whereas I am not untrue to her ... I have deserted her.'

Turning away from him, she began to dress. She had regained her freedom of movement and her disingenuous tolerance. The palest of pink frocks now hid from view the woman who, a moment since, had pressed her last stitch of clothing to her bosom, as though to a wound.

She had recovered, too, her buoyant determination, her desire to live and hold sway, her prodigious and feminine aptitude for happiness. Chéri despised her afresh; but a moment came when the rays of the evening sun, shining through her transparent pink dress, outlined the shape of a young woman who no longer bore any semblance to the wounded Circassian: a heaven-aspiring form, as supple and vigorous as a serpent about to strike.

'I can still hurt her, but how quickly she recovers! In this house, too, I am no longer needed, no longer expected. She has gone far beyond me, and is going further: I am, the old creature would say, her "first turn". It's now for me to follow her example, if only I could. But I can't. And then would I, if I could? Unlike some of us, Edmée has never come up against what one meets only once in a lifetime and is floored by completely. Spéleïeff was fond of saying that, after a really bad crash – which, however, involved no broken bones – some horses would let themselves be killed rather than take the fence again. I am just the same.'

He cast about for further sporting, and rather brutal, metaphors that would make his own fall and misfortunes seem an accident. But he had started his night too early, and, dog-tired, his dreams were haunted by sweet ghosts in sky-blue flounces, and half-remembered figures from the pages of the imperishable literature which finds its way into tawdry love-nests, from tales and poems dedicated to constancy and to lovers undivided in death: writings irresistible to adolescents and time-worn courtesans, who are akin in their credulity and passion for romance.

'THEN she said to me: "I know who's at the back of all this: it's Charlotte again, making mischief about me. ..." "It's no more than you deserve," I told her, "you've only to stop going to see Charlotte as much as you do, and trusting her with all your secrets." She retorted: "I'm a much closer friend of Charlotte's than of Spéleïeff's and I've known her far longer. I assure you Charlotte, Neuilly, bezique, and the child would be a far greater loss to me than Spéleïeff – you can't change the habits of a lifetime." "That doesn't prevent your faith in Charlotte costing you a pretty penny," I said. "Oh! well," was her answer, "what's good is worth paying for." That's her all over, you'll agree: big-hearted and generous but no fool. And with that she went off to dress for the Races – she told me she was going to the Races with a gigolo. ...'

'With me!' Chéri exclaimed bitterly. 'Am I right? It was me?'

'I don't deny it. I simply tell you things as they took place. A white dress – of white crêpe-de-chine – Oriental-looking, edged with blue Chinese embroidery, the very dress you see her in here, in this snapshot, taken at the Races. And nothing will get it out of my head that this man's shoulder you can see behind her is you.'

'Fetch it me!' Chéri ordered.

The old woman got up, pulled out the rusty drawing-pins tacking the photograph to the wall, and brought it back to Chéri. Lolling on the Algerian divan, he raised a tousled head, and, barely running his eyes over it, flung the snapshot across the room.

'When have you seen me wearing a collar that gapes at the back, and a short coat to go to the Races? Come, think again! I don't find that sort of thing at all funny.'

She ventured a tut-tut of timid censure, bent her stiff knees to pick up the photograph, and went on to open the door into the passage.

'Where are you going?'

'I can hear the water for my coffee boiling. I'm going to pour it out.'

'Good. But come back here again.'

She disappeared in a shuffle of rustling taffeta and heelless slippers. Left to himself, Chéri settled his neck against the moquette cushion stamped with Tunisian designs. A new and startlingly bright Japanese kimono, embellished with pink wistaria on a ground of amethyst, had replaced his coat and waistcoat. The fag-end of a too-far-smoked cigarette was almost burning his lips, and his hair, falling fanwise down to the level of his eyebrows, half covered his forehead.

Wearing so feminine and flowered a garment did not make his appearance in any way ambiguous: he merely acquired an ignominious majesty that stamped every feature with its proper value. He seemed bent on death and destruction, and the photograph had flashed like a blade from his hand as he hurled it from him. Hard, delicate bones in his cheeks moved to the rhythm of his working jaws. The whites of his eyes flickered in the darkness round him like the crest of a wave, with the moonbeams interruptedly following its course.

Left alone, however, he let his head sink back against the cushion, and closed his eyes.

'Lord!' exclaimed the Pal, coming back into the room, 'you'll not look more handsome when laid out on your deathbed! I've brought in the coffee. Would you care for some? Such an aroma! It will waft you to the Isles of the Blest.'

'Yes. Two lumps.'

His words were curt, and she obeyed with a humility that suggested, perhaps, a deep subservient pleasure.

'You didn't eat anything for dinner?'

'I had enough.'

He drank his coffee, without moving, supporting himself on one elbow. An Oriental curtain, draped like a canopy, hung from the ceiling directly above the divan, and in its shade lay an ivory and enamel Chéri, robed in exquisite silks, reclining upon an old worn dust-bedraggled rug.

The Pal set out, piece by piece upon a brass-topped table, the coffee-set, an opium lamp capped with a glass cowl, two pipes, the pot of paste, the silver snuff-box used for cocaine, and a flask, which, tight-stoppered as it was, failed to control the cold and treacherously volatile expansion of the ether. To these she added a pack of tarot cards, a case of poker chips, and a pair of spectacles, before settling herself down with the apologetic air of a trained hospital nurse.

'I've already told you', grunted Chéri, 'all that paraphernalia means nothing to me.'

Once again she stretched out her sickly white hands in protestation. In her own home she adopted what she called her 'Charlotte Corday style': hair flowing loose, and wide white linen fichus crossed over her dusty mourning, looking a mixture of decorum and fallen virtue – like a heroine of the Salpêtrière Prison.

'No matter, Chéri. They're just in case. And it does make me so happy to see the whole of my little armoury set out in its proper order under my eyes. The arsenal of dreams! the munitions of ecstasy! the gateway to illusion!'

She nodded her long head and looked up to the ceiling, with the compassionate eyes of a grandmother who ruins herself on toys. Her guest partook of none of her potions. Some sort of physical sense of honour still survived in him, and his disdain for drugs was akin to his distaste for brothels.

For a number of days – he had kept no count of them – he had found his way to this black hole, presided over by an attendant Norn. Ungraciously, and in terms that brooked no argument, he had paid for her food, coffee, and her own liqueurs, and for his personal requirements in the way of cigarettes, fruit, ice, and soft drinks. He had commanded his slave to buy the sumptuous Japanese robe, scents, and expensive soaps. She was moved less by desire for money than by the pleasure of acting as an accomplice. She devoted herself to Chéri with enthusiasm, a revival of her old zeal as a missionary of vice who, with garrulous and culpable alacrity, would divest and bathe a virgin, cook an opium pellet, and pour out intoxicating spirits or ether. This apostolate was fruitless, for her singular guest brought back no paramour, drank soft drinks only, stretched himself on the dusty divan, and delivered only one word of command: 'Talk.'

She did talk, following, she believed, her own fancies; but, now brutally, now subtly, he would direct the muddied meanderings of her reminiscences. She talked like a sewing-woman who comes in by the day, with the continuous, stupefying monotony of creatures whose days are given over to long and sedentary tasks. But she never did any sewing, for she had the aristocratic unpracticalness of a former prostitute. While talking, she would pin a pleat over a hole or stain, and take up again the business of tarot cards and patience. She would put on gloves to grind coffee bought by the charwoman, and then handle greasy cards without turning a hair.

She talked, and Chéri listened to her soporific voice and the shuffle of her felted slippers. He reclined at ease, magnificently robed, in the ill-kept lodging. His guardian dared ask no questions. She knew enough: he was a monomaniac, as his abstemiousness proved. The illness for which she was ministering was mysterious; but it was an illness. She risked asking in, as though from a sense of duty, a very pretty young woman, childish and professionally gay. Chéri paid her neither more nor less attention than he would a puppy, and said to the Pal, 'Are we going to have any more of your fashionable parties?'

She did not require snubbing a second time, and he never had cause to bind her to secrecy. One day she almost hit upon the simple truth, when she proposed asking in two or three of her friends of the good old days; Léa, for instance. He never batted an eyelid.

'Not a soul. Or I'll have to hunt out some better hole.'

A fortnight went by, as funereal in its routine as life in a monastery; but it did not pall on either recluse. During the daytime, the Pal set forth on her old woman's junketings: poker parties, nips of whisky, and poisonous gossip, hole-and-corner gambling-dens, lunches of 'regional dishes' in the stuffy darkness of a Norman or Limousin restaurant. Chéri would arrive with the first shadow of evening, sometimes drenched to the skin. She would recognize the slam of his taxi-door and no longer asked: 'But why do you never come in your motor?'

He would leave after midnight, and usually before daybreak. During his prolonged sessions on the Algerian divan, the Pal sometimes saw him drop off to sleep and remain for an instant or two with his neck twisted against his shoulder, as though caught in a snare. She never slept herself till after his departure, having forgotten the need for repose. Only once, in the small hours of the morning, while he was putting back, meticulously and one by one, the contents of his pockets – key on its chain, note-case, little flat revolver, handkerchief, cigarette-case of green gold – did she dare to ask: 'Doesn't your wife begin to wonder, when you come in so late?'

99

Chéri raised long eyebrows above eyes grown larger from lack of sleep: 'No. Why? She knows perfectly well I've been up to no harm.'

'No child, of course, is easier to manage than you are. ... Shall you be coming again this evening?'

'I don't know. I'll see. Carry on as if I were coming for certain.'

Once more he gazed long at all the lily necks, all the blue eyes, that flowered on one wall of his sanctuary, before he went his way, only to return again, faithfully, some twelve hours later.

By roundabout ways he considered cunning, he would lead the Pal to speak of Léa, then he would clear the narrative of all bawdy asides that might retard it. 'Skip it. Skip it!' Barely bothering to enunciate the words, he relied on the initial sibilants to speed up or curtail the monologue. He would listen only to stories without malice in them, and glorifications of a purely descriptive nature. He insisted upon strict respect for documentary truth and checked his chronicler peevishly. He stocked his mind with dates, colours, materials, and places, and the names of dressmakers.

'What's poplin?' he fired at her point-blank.

'Poplin's a mixture of silk and wool, a dry material ... if you know what I mean; one that doesn't stick to the skin.'

'Yes. And mohair? You said "of white mohair".'

'Mohair is a kind of alpaca, but it hangs better, of course. Léa was afraid to wear lawn in the summer: she maintained that it was best for underwear and handkerchiefs. Her own lingerie was fit for a queen, you'll remember, and in the days when that photograph was taken – yes, that beauty over there with the long legs – they didn't wear the plain underclothes of today. It was frill upon frill, a foam, a flurry of snow; and the drawers, dear boy! they'd have sent your head whirling. ... White Chantilly lace at the sides and black Chantilly in between. Can't you just see the effect? But *can* you imagine it?'

'Revolting,' thought Chéri, 'revolting. Black Chantilly in between. A woman doesn't wear black Chantilly in between simply to please herself. In front of whose eyes did she wear them? For whom?'

He could see Léa's gesture as he entered her bathroom or boudoir – the furtive gesture as she drew her wrap across her body. He could see the chaste self-confidence of her rosy body as she lay naked in the bath, with the water turned to milk by some essence or other. ... 'But, for others, she wore drawers of Chantilly lace. ...'

He kicked one of the hay-stuffed moquette cushions to the floor. 'Are you too warm, Chéri?'

'No. Let me have another look at that photo ... the large framed one. Tilt the what's-its-name of your lamp up a bit ... a bit more ... that's it!'

Abandoning his usual circumspection, he applied a searching eye to the study of every detail that was new to him, and almost refreshing. 'A high-waisted belt with cameos! ... Never saw that about the place. And boots like buskins! Was she wearing tights? No, of course not, her toes are bare. Revolting. ...'

'At whose house did she wear that costume?'

'I don't rightly remember. ... A reception at the club, I believe ... or at Molier's.'

He handed back the frame at arm's length, to all appearances disdainful and bored. He left shortly afterwards, under an overcast sky, towards the close of a night that smelt of wood smoke and dankness.

He was deteriorating physically and took no account of it. He was losing weight through eating and sleeping too little, walking and smoking too much, thus bartering his obvious vigour for a lightness, an apparent return to youth, which the light of day repudiated. At home, he lived as he pleased, welcoming or running away from guests and callers. All that they knew of him was his name, his almost petrified good looks fined down little by little under an accusing chisel, and the inconceivable ease with which he would ignore them.

So he eked out his peaceful and carefully regimented despair until the last days of October. Then, one afternoon, he was seized by a fit of hilarity, because he caught a glimpse of his wife's unsuspected terror. His whole face lit up with the merriment of a man impervious to all feeling. 'She thinks I'm mad. What luck!'

His merriment was short-lived: for, on thinking it over, he came to the conclusion that, where the brute and the madman are concerned, the brute wins every time. She was frightened of the madman; otherwise would she not have stood her ground, biting her lips and forcing back her tears, in order to worst the brute?

'I am no longer even considered wicked,' he thought bitterly. 'And that's because I am no longer wicked. Oh! the harm the woman I left has done to me! Yet others left her, and she left others. ... How, I wonder, does Bacciocchi exist at the present time? or Septfons, Spéleïeff, and all the rest of them? But what have we got in common, I and the rest of them? She called me "little bourgeois" because I counted the bottles in the cellar. "Little bourgeois", "faithful heart", "great lover" – those were her names for me – those were my real names: and, though she watched my departure with tears glistening in her eyes, she is still herself, Léa, who prefers old age to me, who sits in the corner by the fire counting over on her fingers: "I've had What's-his-name, and Thingummy-bob, and Chéri, and So-and-so ..." I thought she belonged to me alone, and never perceived that I was only one among her lovers. Is there anyone left, now, that I am not ashamed of?'

Hardened by now to the exercise of impassivity, he sought to endure the capricious hauntings of such thoughts with resignation, and to be worthy of the devil by which he was possessed. Proud and dry-eyed, with a lighted match held between steady fingers, he looked sideways at his mother, well aware of her watchful eye. Once his cigarette was alight, with a little encouragement he would have strutted like a peacock in front of an invisible public, and taunted his tormentors with a 'Good, isn't it?' In a confused way, the strength born of his dissimulation and resistance was gathering in his inmost self. He was beginning now to enjoy his extreme state of detachment, and dimly perceived that an emotional storm could be just as valuable and refreshing as a lull, and that in it he might discover the wisdom which never came to him in calmer moods. As a child, Chéri frequently had taken advantage of a genuine fit of temper, by changing it into a peevishness that would bring him what he wanted. Today he was fast approaching the point at which, having attained to a definite state of unhappiness, he could rely on it to settle everything.

One gusty, wind-swept, September afternoon, with leaves sailing straight across the sky – an afternoon of blue rifts in the clouds and scattered raindrops – Chéri felt an urge to visit his dark retreat and its attendant, garbed in black, with a touch of white on the chest like a scavenging cat. He was feeling buoyant, and avid for confidences, though these would be sickly, like the fruit of the arbutus and as prickly leaved. Words and phrases of special though ill-defined significance kept running in his head: 'Her monogram embroidered in hair on all her lingerie, dear boy, in golden hairs from her own head ... faery handicraft! And, did I tell you, her masseuse used to pluck the hairs from the calves of her leg, one by one. ...'

He turned round and left the window. He found Charlotte on a chair looking thoughtfully up at him; and in the restless waters of her great eyes he saw the formation of a prodigious, rounded, crystalline, glistening sphere which detached itself from the bronzed pupil, and then vanished, evaporating in the heat of her flushed cheek. Chéri felt flattered and cheered. 'How kind of her! She's weeping for me.'

An hour later, he found his ancient accomplice at her post. But she was wearing some sort of parson's hat, bunched up with shiny black ribbon, and she held out to him a sheet of blue paper, which he waved aside.

'What's that? ... I haven't the time. Tell me what's written on it.'

The Pal lifted puzzled eyes to his: 'It's my mother.'

'Your mother? You're joking.'

She did her best to appear offended. 'I'm not joking at all. Please respect the departed! She is dead.' And she added, by way of an excuse, 'She was eighty-three!'

'Congratulations. Are you going out?'

'No; I'm going away.'

'Where to?'

'To Tarascon, and from there I take a little branch line train that puts me down at ...'

'For how long?'

'Four or five days ... at least. There's the solicitor to be seen about the will, because my younger sister –'

He burst out, hands to heaven: 'A sister now! Why not four children into the bargain?' He was conscious of the unexpectedly high-pitched tone of his voice and controlled it. 'Good, very well. What d'you expect me to do about it? Be off, be off. ...'

'I was going to leave word for you. I'm catching the 7.30.'

'Catch the 7.30.'

'The time of the funeral service is not mentioned in the telegram: my sister speaks only of the laying out, the climate down there is very hot, they'll have to get through it very quickly, only the business side can keep me there, and over that one has no control.'

'Of course, of course.'

He was walking to and fro, from the door to the wall with the photographs and back to the door again, and in doing so he knocked against a squashed old travelling-bag. The coffee-pot and cups were steaming on the table.

'I made you your coffee, come what might. ...'

'Thanks.'

They drank standing up, as at a station, and the chill of departure gripped Chéri by the throat and made his teeth chatter secretly.

'Goodbye, then, dear boy,' said the Pal. 'You may be sure that I'll hurry things as much as I can.'

'Goodbye – pleasant journey.'

They shook hands, and she did not dare to kiss him. 'Won't you stay here for a little while?'

He looked all round in great agitation. 'No. No.'

'Take the key, then?'

'Why should I?'

'You're at home here. You've fallen into the habit of it. I've told Maria to come every day at five and light a good fire and get the coffee ready. ... So take my key, won't you? ...'

With a limp hand he took the key, and it struck him as enormous. Once outside, he longed to throw it away or take it back to the concierge.

The old woman took courage on her way between her own door and the street, loading him with instructions as she might a child of twelve.

'The electric-light switch is on your left as you go in. The kettle is always on the gas-stove in the kitchen, and all you have to do is to put a match to it. And your Japanese robe – Maria has her instructions to leave it folded at the head of the divan and the cigarettes in their usual place.'

Chéri nodded affirmation once or twice, with the look of cour-ageous unconcern of a schoolboy on the last morning of the holidays. And, when he was alone, it did not occur to him to make fun of his old retainer with the dyed hair, who had placed the proper value both on the last prerogatives of the dead and on the little pleasures of one whom all had now deserted.

The following morning he awoke from an indecipherable dream, in which a crush of people were all running in the same direction. Though he saw only their backs, each was known to him. As they hurried by, he identified his mother, Léa – unaccountably naked, and out of breath – Desmond, the Pal, and young Maudru ... Edmée was the only one to turn and smile at him, with the grating little smile of a marten. 'But it's the marten Ragut caught in the Vosges!' Chéri cried out in his dream, and this discovery pleased him immeasurably. Then he checked and recounted all the one-way runners, saying over to himself: 'There's one missing. ... There's one missing. ...' Once out of his dream, on this side of awakening, it came to him that the one missing was none other than himself: 'I must get back into it. ...' But the efforts of exerting every limb, like an insect caught on fly-paper, served only to widen the bar of blue between his eyelids, and he emerged into that real world in which he was frittering away his time and his strength. He stretched out his legs, and bathed them in a fresh, cool part of the sheets. 'Edmée must have got up some time ago.'

He was surprised to see beneath the window a new garden of marguerites and heliotrope, for in his memory there was only a summer garden of blue and pink. He rang, and the sound of the bell brought to life a maid whose face was unfamiliar.

'Where is Henriette?'

'I've taken her place, sir.'

'Since when?'

'Why – for the last month, sir.'

He ejaculated an 'Ah!' as much as to say, 'That explains every-thing.'

'Where's your mistress?'

'Madame is just coming, sir. Madame is ready to go out.'

Edmée, indeed, did appear, as large as life, but stopped just inside the door in so marked a manner that Chéri was secretly amused. He allowed himself the pleasure of upsetting his wife a little by exclaiming, 'But it's Ragut's marten!' and watching her pretty eyes waver under his gaze.

'Fred, I ...'

'Yes, you're going out. I never heard you get up.'

She coloured slightly. 'There's nothing extraordinary in that. I've been sleeping so badly these last few nights, that I've had a bed made up on the divan in the boudoir. You're not doing anything special today, are you?'

'But I am,' he replied darkly.

'Is it important?'

'Very important.' He took his time, and finished on a lighter note: 'I'm going to have my hair cut.'

'But will you be back for luncheon?'

'No; I'll have a cutlet in Paris. I've made an appointment at Gustave's for a quarter past two. The man who usually comes to cut my hair is ill.'

He was childishly courteous, the lie flowering effortlessly on his lips. Because he was lying, his mouth took on its boyhood mould – poutingly provocative and rounded for a kiss. Edmée looked at him with an almost masculine satisfaction.

'You're looking well this morning, Fred. ... I must fly.'

'Are you catching the 7.30?'

She stared at him, struck dumb, and fled so precipitately that he was still laughing when the front door slammed behind her.

'Ah! that does me good,' he sighed. 'How easy it is to laugh when you no longer expect anything from anyone. ...' Thus, while he was dressing, did he discover for himself the nature of asceticism, and the tuneless little song he hummed through pursed lips kept him company like a silly young nun.

He went down to a Paris he had forgotten. The crowd upset his dubious emotional balance, now so dependent on a crystalline vacuity and the daily routine of suffering.

In the Rue Royale he came face to face with his own full-length reflection at the moment when the brightness of noon broke through the rain-clouds. Chéri wasted no thoughts on this crude new self-portrait, which stood out sharply against a background of news-vendors and shopgirls, flanked by jade necklaces and silver fox furs. The fluid feeling in his stomach, which he compared to a speck of lead bobbing about inside a celluloid ball, must come, he thought, from lack of sustenance, and he took refuge in a restaurant.

With his back to a glass partition, screened from the light of day, he lunched off selected oysters, fish, and fruit. Some young women sitting not far away had no eyes for him, and this gave him a pleasant feeling, like that of a chilly bunch of violets laid on closed eyelids. But the smell of his coffee suddenly brought home the need to rise and keep the appointment of which this smell was an urgent re-minder. Before obeying the summons, he went to his hairdresser's, held out his hands to be manicured, and slipped off into a few moments' inestimable repose, while expert fingers substituted their will for his.

The enormous key obstructed his pocket. 'I won't go, I won't go! ...' To the cadence of some such insistent, meaningless refrain, he found his way without mishap to the Avenue de Villiers. His clumsy fumbling round the lock and the rasp of the key made his heart beat momentarily faster, but the cheerful warmth in the passage calmed his nerves.

He went forward cautiously, lord of this empire of a few square feet, which he now owned but did not know. The useless daily arrangement of the armoury had been laid out on the table by the well-trained charwoman, and an earthenware coffee-pot stood in the midst of charcoal embers already dying under the velvet of warm ashes. Methodically, Chéri emptied his pockets and set out one by one his cigarette-case, the huge key, his own small key, the flat revolver, his note-case, handkerchief, and watch; but when he had put on his Japanese robe, he did not lie down on the divan. With the silent curiosity of a cat he opened doors and peered into cupboards. His peculiar prudishness shrank back before a primitive but dis-tinctively feminine lavatory. The bedroom, all bed and little else, also was decorated in the mournful shade of red that seems to settle in on those of declining years; it smelt of old bachelors and eau-de-

Cologne. Chéri returned to the drawing-room. He switched on the two wall lamps and the beribboned chandelier. He listened to faint far-away sounds and, now that he was alone for the first time in this poor lodging, began trying out on himself the influence of its previous inmates – birds of passage or else dead. He thought he heard and recognized a familiar footstep, a slipshod, shambling old animal pad-pad, then shook his head: 'It can't be hers. She won't be back for a week, and when she does come back, what will there be left for me in this world? I'll have ...'

Inwardly he listened to the Pal's voice, the worn-out voice of a tramp. 'But wait till I finish the story of the famous slanging-match between Léa and old Mortier at the Races. Old Mortier thought that with the aid of a little publicity in *Gil Blas* he would get all he wanted out of Léa. Oh! la la, my pretties, what a donkey he made of himself! She drove out to Longchamp – a dream of blue – as statuesque as a goddess, in her victoria drawn by a pair of piebalds. ...'

He raised his hand towards the wall in front of him, where so many blue eyes were smiling, where so many swan-necks were preening themselves above imperturbable bosoms. '... I'll have all this. All this, and nothing more. It's true, perhaps, that this is a good deal. I've found her again, by a happy chance, found her here on this wall. But I've found her, only to lose her again for ever. I am still held up, like her, by these few rusty nails, by these pins stuck in slantwise. How much longer can this go on? Not very long. And then, knowing myself as I do, I'm afraid I shall demand more than this. I may suddenly cry out: "I want her! I must have her! Now! at this very moment!" Then what will become of me?'

He pushed the divan closer to the illustrated wall and there lay down. And as he lay there, all the Léas, with their downward gazing eyes, seemed to be showing concern for him: 'But they only *seem* to be looking down at me, I know perfectly well. When you sent me away, my Nounoune, what did you think there was left for me after you? Your noble action cost you little – you knew the worth of a Chéri – your risk was negligible. But we've been well punished, you and I: you, because you were born so long before me, and I, because I loved you above all other women. You're finished now, you have found your consolation – and what a disgrace that is! – whereas I ...'

As long as people say, "There was the War," I can say "There was Léa." Léa, the War ... I never imagined I'd dream of either of them again, yet the two together have driven me outside the times I live in. Henceforth, there is nowhere in the world where I can occupy more than half a place. ...'

He pulled the table nearer to consult his watch. 'Half past five. The old creature won't be back here for another week. And this is the first day. Supposing she were to die on the way?'

He fidgeted on his divan, smoked, poured himself out a cup of lukewarm coffee. 'A week. All the same, I mustn't ask too much of myself. In a week's time ... which story will she be telling me? I know them off by heart – the one about the Four-in-Hand Meet, the one about the slanging-match at Longchamp, the one about the final rupture – and when I've heard every one, every twist and turn of them, what will there be left? Nothing, absolutely nothing. In a week's time, this old woman – and I'm already so impatient for her, she might be going to give me an injection – this old woman will be here, and ... and she'll bring me nothing at all.'

He lifted beseeching eyes to his favourite photograph. Already this speaking likeness filled him with less resentment, less ecstasy, less heartbreak. He turned from side to side on the hard mattress, unable to prevent his muscles from contracting, like a man who aches to jump from a height, but lacks the courage.

He worked himself up till he groaned aloud, repeating over and over again 'Nounoune', to make himself believe he was frantic. But he fell silent, ashamed, for he knew very well that he did not need to be frantic to pick up the little flat revolver from the table. Without rising, he experimented in finding a convenient position. Finally he lay down with his right arm doubled up under him. Holding the weapon in his right hand, he pressed his ear against the muzzle, which was buried in the cushions. At once his arm began to grow numb, and he realized that if he did not make haste his tingling fingers would refuse to obey him. So he made haste, whimpering muffled complaints as he completed his task, because his forearm was hurting, crushed under the weight of his body. He knew nothing more, beyond the pressure of his forefinger on a little lever of tempered steel.

Colette

CLAUDINE MARRIED

'She said what no man could have said, and she spoke of sensations and feelings as nobody had spoken of them before'
Andre Maurois

Following the excitement of a shared life in Paris Claudine's marriage to the distinguished Renaud has settled into a stale pattern of bickering conversations and mutual inattention. Just as Claudine begins to fear herself confined to a stifled existence a chance meeting with a friend's wife, the beautiful Rézi, draws her into an impassioned and heartbreaking affair.

In *Claudine Married* Claudine pits her uniquely sensuous spirit against the challenges of married life and the conflicts of forbidden love in one of Colette's most moving and powerful novels.

'Her sense of comedy is exuberant; her understanding of character...is profound...From her imagination images rush profusely forth like bees from a hive...nudes from the staircase of the Moulin Rouge, platitudes from statesmen, or paintings from Picasso'
Raymond Mortimer

V

VINTAGE

Colette

CLAUDINE IN PARIS

'Everything that Colette touched became human...'
The Times

At the age of seventeen Claudine is in despair having left her beloved Montigny for a new life in Paris. Comforted by her devoted maid Mélie, her slug-obsessed Papa, and the trustworthy cat Fanchette, Claudine's instinctive curiosity gradually leads to an awakened interest in the city.

Ruthless, impetuous and chastely sensual Claudine records her witty observations and adventures amongst the intriguing characters that surround her, evoking the glamour and excitement of Parisian life.

Written with striking realism *Claudine in Paris* is an inspiring portrait of a precocious young girl on the brink of transformation into a woman for her, and our, time.

'Her sense of comedy is exuberant; her understanding of character - within her chosen limits - is profound...From her imagination images rush profusely forth like bees from a hive, pollen from poplars, smoke from a cigarette, nudes from the staircase of the Moulin Rouge, platitudes from statesmen, or paintings from Picasso'
Raymond Mortimer

Colette

GIGI
AND
THE CAT

'Her sensual prose style made her one of the great writers of
20th-century France'
New York Times Book Review

In these two superb stories of the politics of love, Colette is
at her witty, instinctive best. Gigi is being educated in the
skills of the Courtesan: to choose cigars, to eat lobster, to
enter a world where a woman's chief weapon is her body.
However, when it comes to the question of Gaston
Lachaille, very rich and very bored, Gigi does not want to
obey the rules.

In 'The Cat', a wonderful story of burgeoning sexuality and
blossoming love, an exquisite strong-minded Russian Blue is
struggling for mastery of Alain with his seductive fiancée,
Camille.

VINTAGE

Also available in Vintage

Colette

CHANCE ACQUAINTANCES AND JULIE DE CARNEILHAN

'Her sensual prose style made her one of the great writers of 20th-century France'
New York Times Book Review

Set in pre-war Paris, *Julie de Carneilhan* tells of the complex relationship between proud but impoverished Julie and her former husband, the Comte d'Espivant, who has remarried a wealth widow. *Julie de Carneilhan* was the last full-length novel Colette was to write as was as close a reckoning with the elements of her second marriage as she ever allowed herself.

In *Chance Acquaintances* Colette visits a health resort accompanied only by her cat. While there, she befriends the handsome Gerard Haume and his invalid wife Antoinette, and is unwittingly caught up in the mysterious and disturbing events which befall them.

VINTAGE

Colette

CHÉRI

'I devoured *Chéri* at a gulp. What a wonderful subject and with what intelligence, mastery and understanding of the least-admitted secrets of the flesh'
André Gide

Cheri, first published in 1920, is considered Colette's finest novel. Exquisitely handsome, spoilt and sardonic, Chéri is the only son of a wealthy courtesan, a contemporary of Léa, the magnificent and talented woman who for six years has devoted herself to his amorous education.

When a rich marriage is arranged for Chéri, Léa reluctantly decides their relationship must end. Chéri, despite his apparent detachment, is haunted by memories of Léa; alienated from his wife, his family and his surroundings, he retreats into a fantasy world made up of dreams and the past, a world from which there is only one route of escape.

In her portrait of the fated love affair between a very young man and a middle-aged woman, Colette achieved a peak in her earthy, sensuous and utterly individual art. *Chéri* caused considerable controversy both in its choice of setting – the fabulous *demi-monde* of the Parisian courtesans – and in its portrayal of Chéri.

VINTAGE